HE'S HERE!

My Elisa!
Thank you so much
for EVERYTHING!!!
Love you Always,

Lisa Hodorowych

More Books by (or featuring) Lisa Hodorovych

The Disappearance

Giant Bug Cinema: A Monster Kids' Guide

An author's "bread and butter" are the reviews left by amazing readers, like you, whether good or bad. After reading any of my books, please leave a review on Amazon, GoodReads, and/or your social media (please make sure to tag me). Thank you in advance!

HE'S HERE!

Lisa Hodorovych

Quoth the Writer, L.L.C.
Whippany, NJ

Cover Design by Mark Bailey

ISBN (paperback): 979-8-218-19217-4

Printed in the United States of America

To my rock, my favorite, my love, my everything!
We did it again, babe! But we're not done!
Let the fun continue! I love you!

Note from Author

Please be advised, there are scenes of attempted rape, stalking, physical abuse, and manipulation. Read at your discretion.

JANUARY 5th

Just two days ago, Jack and I were sitting in our office in Sacramento, reading an article about the creatures at Lake Minnetaha and learning that something was definitely going on there. Yesterday we drove down and now, we're in Los Angles, hoping to get clearance to go back and do another episode. Unfortunately (or fortunately, depending on how you look at it), with us constantly traveling for the show, this is the only way we'll be able to get out there immediately.

As we sat in a rich lobby on lush leather chairs, waiting to be called in, my mind drifted to Roman, Kaden, and Glen. I reminisced about what I read and thought, "My boys can't be a part of the destruction going on there. They wouldn't even harm a fly. And they were only protecting me when they attacked whoever was trying to get in that one night. Although, the way Roman was talking when they mentioned Nash being tied up was scary and disheartening. But that's also Roman, he's an asshole!"

I silently chortled and shook my head. That's when I felt a nudge on my shoulder. "Ash?"

I snapped out of it and looked at Jack. "Yeah?"

"You okay, babe? Look like you were in deep thought for a second there." He paused. "Thinking about the guys?"

I nodded. "I just keep going back to that article. I know my boys would never do anything like that, but …"

"You can't help but wonder 'what if?'"

I glared at him. "Okay, since when did you become Chad?!" We both laughed. "But exactly. I mean, what if that serum, or whatever they were injected with, is starting to mess with their minds."

"Don't think like that, babe. Everything is going to be fine," he said, rubbing my back. "And whatever is going on, we'll get to the bottom of it."

I looked at him. "Together?"

He smiled. "Together. Once we get clearance."

As we continued waiting, I started to reminisce about this whole ordeal. The boys leaving, me waiting, me seeing Glen for the first time and falling over that damn rocking chair. I snorted a little, laughing at myself for being so reckless. Jack looked at me. "What was that?"

"Sorry. Just remembering when I fell on my elbow and how embarrassing that was."

He tittered as he rubbed his forehead. "Oh, geez, babe."

I continued laughing at myself as the memories carried on. I remembered when I called Jack and he literally dropped everything to help me. I couldn't help but smile as my heart fluttered with that memory. But then I thought of something. *Wait a minute, he didn't ask for permission to come to the cabin then! Why are we here?*

I panned over to him, my brow furrowed. "Jack?"

"Yes, baby?" He looked at me and flinched a little from the look at my face. "What's wrong?"

"Why are we here?"

He was utterly confused. "I'm sorry?"

In a staccato rhythm, I repeated, "Why are we here?"

He kind of looked around, completely lost as to why I was asking that question. "Uh … because we're looking to get the okay to go back to Lake Minnetaha, to go back to the cabin."

"But why when two years ago you dropped everything to help me."

The realization hit him square in the face and his head just sagged. "Babe, that was a different time. We weren't tied down by 'rules and regulations' from the network. They allowed us to do whatever we wanted to get the show started."

"Oh." I understood, but I wasn't totally satisfied with the answer.

Even though I looked away from him, Jack could still read my body language. If there's anybody that knows me all too well, it is definitely my husband. He grabbed my hand, interlocking our fingers, and said, "Baby, I know you see me as a massive kiss ass, but I don't want to mess up what we got. We have something really good happening right now with this show. I'm sorry, but ..."

I met his eyes. "No, it's okay, babe. You're right; I just want to get out there as soon as possible."

"And we will." He kissed my hand and for a hot second my favorite feeling came back. It felt like it was just the two of us. We pressed our foreheads together. I closed my eyes, taking in the moment, until the door to the main office opened. We panned over to see Melanie, Mr. Robinson's secretary, standing in the doorway. "Hey, Jack. Hey, Ashlynn. Mr. Robinson will see you now."

We stood up and walked through the doors, following Melanie down a hallway. Since I've gotten friendly with her over the past year or so—I talk to her more than Mr. Robinson—I asked, "How were your holidays, Mel?"

"Good, thank you. Spent Christmas Eve with Garrett's

family and then Christmas Day with mine. You?"

"Crazy, but good. We hosted this year, so mine and Jack's parents came over."

"Oh, goodness. How many times were you asked when they're going to be grandparents?"

Jack and I looked at each other and rolled our eyes. If either of us got a freaking penny every time we were asked when we were going to have a baby, we would be millionaires now. I answered, "Actually, Jack's parents were very good. They only asked once. My mom, on the other hand, I lost count after the first day." We all laughed.

At the end of the hall, we reached another wooden door that was left wide open, muttered chat coming from it. Jack and I walked in, and as we did, Mr. Robinson looked up, smiled broadly, and exclaimed, "Jack, my dear boy!"

Let me explain something here. Mr. Robinson is a British man who is in his late sixties/early seventies and *loves* Jack. He has seen him as a son and has been his biggest supporter since the very beginning. As much as I truly appreciate that, at the same time if Mr. Robinson told Jack to jump, he would ask, "How high?"

Every time we meet with him—either in person, over the phone, or virtually—Jack reminds me to be on my best behavior because he doesn't want to mess anything up or upset "the boss." As he said earlier, he's "a massive ass kisser." It's a little ridiculous, but I roll with it.

Mr. Robinson got up and walked over to us. He embraced Jack like he hadn't seen him in years. "How have you been? Everything going well?"

He let go and held Jack at arm's length. Jack replied, "Yes, everything is fine. Thank you, Mr. Robinson."

"Good, glad to hear." Then he looked over at me. "Ashlynn, my dear girl." He came over and hugged me. "How are you doing, love?"

"I'm well, Mr. Robinson. And yourself?"

We let go. "Pretty good. Any children from my favorite couple yet?"

I rubbed my tummy. "No, not yet." *Thanks for the reminder, jerk!*

His mustached lip fell into a frown. "Well, please don't let me wait forever on being a granddad again."

Granddad?! Who the hell said you would be called granddad?!

We laughed. Jack, wrapping his arm around my shoulders, replied, "No, sir, we won't."

Oh, of course! Mr. Kiss Ass must've given him the impression! Thanks, babe!

Mr. Robinson's smile came back. "Please, sit," he gestured to a long, beautifully polished, wooden table placed in the middle of the room—which reminded me of a library—and a couple of very comfortable leather chairs. Lining the table on both sides were more execs. Some I've met maybe once or twice before, but most I had no clue who they were.

We all went and sat down. As we did, Mr. Robinson explained to his fellow execs, "Chaps, for those of you who don't know, this is Jack Graives. He's a cryptozoologist who, before starting the show, was working on a book about obscure creatures." He looked over at Jack. "By the way, how's that book coming along, Jackie?"

I could tell he was slightly embarrassed. Jack had been working on that book for the past decade or so and is still nowhere close to being done. But he smiled and said, "It's coming along, sir."

"Fantastic." He looked back at his cronies. "Then he came up with an idea to travel around the world and look for these creatures. Well, when I heard about this, I had to snatch it up for the network. You guys know how much that stuff intrigues me." They all chuckled, mumbled, and nodded their heads. "Now that show is one of the top ones on our network."

Jack, being the amazing brownnoser he is, said, "Well, if it wasn't for your kindness, support, and faith in me, Mr. Robinson, this wouldn't be happening."

I actually threw up in my mouth a little when he said that. Yes, I was probably the same way with Mr. Schneider, but something about Mr. Robinson just rubs me the wrong way.

Mr. Robinson leaned forward, grabbed him by the shoulder, and said, "Aw, my dear boy, it's my pleasure." He let go and then looked at me. "And his beautiful wife, Ashlynn is his longtime love. They've known each other since they were little and are now happily married for ..."

"One year," I responded. "I guess you can say we're still in the newlywed phase."

These guys, once again, chuckled, mumbled, and nodded their heads. *Uh, am I surrounded by robots?!*

Mr. Robinson carried on, "Beautiful. Now, what brings you two to my humble abode?"

"Humble abode?!" It's your freaking office! Come on!

Jack started, "Well, sir, we were hoping to head back to Lake Minnetaha, Washington to do a 'revisit' episode, if you will."

Mr. Robinson pondered for a moment. "Hm ... that's not a bad idea, but may I ask why? Is there a new development?"

I answered, "Yes, sir. There have been more sightings and some destruction in Lake Minnetaha and its surrounding towns."

His eyes widened. "Fascinating. Now, Ms. Ashlynn, if you wouldn't mind, would you explain to my chaps here what exactly we're talking about. I know some of them are bad boys and don't watch the network."

My mind screamed, "How do you not watch the shows that help you make millions of dollars?! What the hell is wrong with you?!"

I tried *so hard* to hide what I was thinking, but my face must've shown it because Mr. Robinson said, "Trust me, my dear, I've thought the same thing you're thinking."

I blushed. *Damn! I really need to work on my poker face!*

He added, "So, please," and gestured toward everyone, as if giving me the room.

I took a deep breath in. As I released it, I explained, "A little over a year ago, while I was vacationing in Lake Minnetaha, Washington, I saw something in the woods. It stood somewhere between six and seven feet tall, its skin almost looked charred, and it had these fire-red eyes. I honestly thought I was losing my mind when I first saw it, but then I kept on seeing it. And there was one time it got really close to my cabin, scratching the …" I almost used a "curse" word, but I refrained myself, "… heck out of it. Around that time is when I called Jack, and I guess you can say he came to my rescue."

I looked at him and smiled. He smiled back with those loving eyes of his. That's when one of the execs asked, "So, what did it turn out to be?"

We looked at the exec and then back at each other before

Jack replied, "We're not a hundred percent sure. We've found more than one and they're definitely something new, something not written about in any book, as of yet."

"Exactly, 'as of yet,' Jackie Boy!" Mr. Robinson exclaimed. "You'll be the first when your book comes out!"

Jack smirked, trying to hide his embarrassment. "That's right, sir."

"But are they like Bigfoot? Like a giant ape?" another exec asked.

I panned over to him and answered, "No, they're …" I paused, pondering what the hell I was going to say. "They're like mutants."

My heart sank when I said that. I couldn't tell them the truth and we never classified them on the show. All we said was, "These creatures are something previously unseen and unprecedented." But I had this jerk-off asking me what they were, so that's the answer I came up with in the moment. I hated myself for saying it, but, again, I *had* to hide my emotions.

Then a voice chimed in from the end of the table. "Like the characters from *X-men*?"

We all looked down the table and saw a young man, probably around the same age as Jack and me, with his hand slightly raised and curiosity in his eyes. I replied, "Not exactly. More in the realm of *Incredible Hulk*."

He smirked, understanding what I was talking about, and nodded while everyone else around us was confused. *Well, if you maybe turned on a TV or poked your nose into a comic, you would know what we're saying!*

The young man continued, "If that's the case, maybe they're human and maybe there's a cure to help them."

Before I could answer, Mr. Robinson stated, "Well, that would be boring."

Yeah, we don't want to put anything boring on your network, God forbid!

The thing is, I did think about trying to find a cure, but I'm no scientist. I wouldn't even know where to begin on something like that. Yeah, I could probably talk to a scientist or a chemist or whomever would understand what I'm looking for, but how do I explain why I need this cure? "Yes, can you help me? My brother and two best friends were transformed into these creatures, and I want to change them back."

How many movies have you seen with someone saying something similar and *no one* believing them? That's how I feel. I'm just in no mood to be laughed at or ridiculed.

Mr. Robinson resumed, "Well, let's take a look at the schedule and figure out what we can do." He pressed a button on the intercom box next to him. "Melanie, can you bring me the schedule for *Searching for the Truth*, please?"

"Absolutely. One moment, Mr. Robinson."

"Thanks, love."

I interjected, "I'm sorry, sir, but we were hoping to go out there as soon as possible."

His face creased. "Hm … don't you have a full schedule ahead of you?"

"I believe we do, sir, but we're hoping to maybe move something or take something out."

He became a little irritated. "Well, it's not that simple, my dear. May I ask why the rush?"

Jack and I looked at each other. His eyes were screaming, "Don't say anything! Don't say anything!"

I looked back at Mr. Robinson and replied, "Because my

family's cabin is out there, and like I stated earlier, we've been reading more and more about these creatures invading that area, so I want to make sure it's okay."

Mr. Robinson visibly relaxed. "Oh, that's right. How can I forget about that beautiful cabin? Well, that's understandable, my dear, but …" he waved Melanie in, and she handed him a binder. "Thanks, love." He opened it and started flipping through. "Let's see here …"

After a little bit of scanning through, he picked up his head and said to us, "So you do have a full schedule through April/May, which will set you up for summer programming. And then, we won't have you back on the road until probably September, as long as all goes well with your ratings. I'm sorry, Ashlynn, but it looks like September is the earliest we can do."

I became upset. "Okay, so why can't we go in May after our last taping?"

In a stern, matter-of-fact voice, he replied, "Because that's when you're off and you won't have our backing."

That's when my Italian, New York bitch came out, a little. "Do we really need your backing in order to do this episode?"

Jack whipped his head around, his eyes wide with shock and anger. "Ashlynn!"

Mr. Robinson laughed. "No, Jack, it's okay. She's got moxie and I love it. She has every right to ask that question and the answer is no, you don't … unless, of course, you want to lose the show."

Jack leered at me. *Crap!* I could feel my face becoming redder and redder from embarrassment. Mr. Robinson added, "However, I do understand your situation and since you are my favorite couple, I will give you my blessing. If you need any help with anything, let me know and I will see what I can do."

I twinkled with joy. "Thank you so much, Mr. Robinson. I truly appreciate it and we won't let you down."

He smiled just as bright. "Aw, how can I say 'no' to that face."

I blushed. His "buddies" chuckled, nodded, and mumbled once again. *Seriously! I'm about to look under the table and see if y'all even have legs!*

Then the young man who compared our situation to *X-men* interrupted us. "Sir, I'll type up a letter stating what was discussed today for you and Mrs. Graives to sign. That way it's legally-binding."

Mr. Robinson sighed as his smile faded. "Yes, thank you for that reminder, Riley." He looked at me. "Here's a little lesson for you, Ms. Ashlynn: never do a verbal agreement. Do you know why you should never do that?"

I became tense. I shook my head. "No, why?"

"Because it can come back and bite you in the arse." He laughed, which prompted me to laugh, which then prompted Jack and everyone else in the room to laugh.

After a moment, we composed ourselves and Jack said, "I think we've taken up enough of your time, Mr. Robinson, and we have a lot of planning and traveling to do."

"That you do." He stood up as we did. "It was good to see you, my boy." He gave Jack another big bear hug.

Jack, once again, reciprocated. "It was great seeing you, too, sir."

They let go of each other and Mr. Robinson came over to me. "And my dear, sweet Ashlynn, always a pleasure."

We hugged each other. "Thank you, sir, for everything."

"My pleasure, love. And good luck with this upcoming

season; I'm excited to see what you find."

We let go of each other as I said, "Thanks again. Take care."

As we walked out of the room, Mr. Robinson shouted, "And don't forget, make me a granddad soon!"

We all laughed while I thought, "Yeah, you're lucky if the baby calls you uncle!"

****

Getting onto the elevator, I joked, "I don't know who wants us to have a baby more, Mr. Robinson or my mom."

Jack chuckled. "Maybe we can try again tonight?" he asked, wrapping his hand around my hip and pulling me in closer.

I smirked. "Maybe."

He let go of me and his tone changed. "But seriously, babe, you need to watch what you say in front of these men. Our very lives are at stake and one wrong word could cost us everything."

I scowled at him. "And you think I don't know that."

"No, but at the same time …"

"At the same time, my brothers' lives are in danger and because of this show …"

"You mean the same one that has afforded us the house we live in and the food we eat."

I was taken aback by what he said. "So you're going to throw that in my face now?"

His expression dimmed. He knew he messed up. "Shit, babe, I'm …"

I put my hand up. "No, you're right. You were right when I asked you, no, I *begged* you not to use the episode with my boys since I realized it was them who were the creatures. And you told me what exactly?"

Defeated, he mumbled, "It would be a great episode that would put us on the map."

I continued, almost screaming at him I was so furious, "Which it did, so thank you so much for making me do something I wasn't 100% comfortable with. And now you're right, once again. I'll call up Mr. Robinson and apologize for my actions and tell him the episode can wait until September or next year or whenever we're available to do it. My brothers' lives can wait."

As the elevator stopped and the doors opened, I looked him square in the eyes and said, "You better hope and pray we don't find their dead bodies when we do," and stormed out of the elevator.

I … was … pissed!

The ride back was so quiet you could hear a pin drop in the freaking car. When we reached the hotel, Jack stopped in front of the main door and said in a stoic voice, "I need to run a couple of errands. I'll be back later."

I just said, "Okay," got out of the car, slammed the door, and marched into the hotel and to our room. I went in and paced back and forth for God knows how long, muttering, "I can't believe he fucking said that to me! Who the hell does he think he is?" I lowered my voice to imitate his. "'You mean the same one that has afforded us the house we live in and the food we eat.' What an asshole!"

After pacing so much that I made myself dizzy, I plopped onto the couch and waited for my vision to right itself. "And this is making things *so* much worse! Nice job, Ash!"

I took a couple of deep breaths and placed my head in between my legs until I felt better. After a moment or two, I straightened myself up and, thankfully, the room wasn't spinning anymore. I looked over to my right and saw the remote for the TV. "All right, let's try escaping reality for a bit."

I flipped through, trying to find something good to watch, only to find an episode of *Searching for the Truth*. "Oh, of fucking course!"

I continued switching channels, but when I couldn't find anything else to watch, I decided to just put it on. "Fine, you win again!" I exclaimed to Jack on the TV screen. I then laughed out loud at myself for yelling at it. "Oh, gosh, Ash, you really are losing it."

As I watched the episode, I realized which one it was. "Oh, this is when we looked into the mermaid in Tennessee."

Moments later, I saw myself in a bikini as I prepared to go snorkeling with Jack to see if we could find anything. "Damn, I look good!" I laughed again. That's when I remembered, "Oh, this is where I got touched by something."

It wasn't long before I was reliving that instant as it went to a commercial, but I will never forget it. Jack, Jerry, and I were treading the water in one area of the lake, going back and forth with Chad about not seeing anything, despite the water being rather clear, when I felt something touch my bad ankle. I said, "I think something just touched me," and then it grabbed me, pulling me under. It wasn't like I felt teeth or a tail wrap around and pull, I literally felt a hand. However, after it did, it immediately let go.

As the show came back on, I was also reminded of what happened next. Both Jack and Jerry immediately dove down after me, but Jerry was filming. He actually caught something swimming away from me that we can't explain. While Jerry was filming underwater, Greg was filming up top from the boat. I watched as Jack grabbed me and pulled me up to the surface and toward the boat. He made sure I was in and safe prior to him getting in. While I coughed from inhaling some water, he caressed my head and back, asking, "Are you okay, baby?"

(By this point, the audience already knows we're husband and wife since in previous episodes, including this one, he's said, "My wife, Ashlynn …," so it's not a "big deal" whenever he calls me "babe," or "baby" on the show now.)

I nodded as I continued coughing up a lung.

"Can I have a towel, please?" Jack demanded. Chad handed him one. Kneeling in front of me, he wrapped it around me and caressed my arms. "You sure you're okay?"

Finally done coughing, I responded, "Yes, I'm fine. I'm okay."

He held my head up and looked me straight in the eyes. "Yeah?"

I smiled. "Yeah."

He rested his forehead on mine, and we stayed like that for a little while as I continued catching my breath. In that moment, I remember my favorite feeling came back. It felt like it was just the two of us and our crew was nowhere in sight.

God I love that feeling!

As the episode continued, I beamed and relaxed, remembering that I married a truly amazing man. We all have our flaws and he's just doing what's best for us and our future.

Almost an hour later, I heard the door unlock. I turned off the TV as Jack entered, wielding a decent-sized paper bag. After closing the door, he walked over to me and said, "Hey."

I looked up at him. "Hey."

"May I?" he asked, pointing to the couch.

"Of course," I responded, scooching over.

He sat down and gently grabbed my hand. "Can you ever forgive me for being such an asshole?"

"Of course, I can. But the question is, can you ever forgive me for being an utter bitch?"

"Of course, my love."

He leaned in, kissed me on my cheek, and hugged me. I reciprocated, squeezing him so tight. "I love you," I whispered into his ear.

"I love you, too."

We let go. He said, "I'm so sorry, babe, for what I said. That was wrong of me."

"But it's the truth. I could've seriously cost us everything with my attitude and I'm sorry about that."

"No, it's okay, babe. I understand where you're coming from, and I know how much the boys mean to you. You would do anything for them, and you have." I felt my cheeks redden a little. If there's anybody (or in this case, group of people) that I love as much as Jack, it's Kaden, Roman, and Glen. Jack continued, "I also know how you can be." We both laughed. "I knew it was only going to be a matter of time before you said something."

I shrugged. "And I'm proud of myself. I could've been *way* worse."

"I know! Did you call Mr. Robinson?"

"No, not yet."

"Good. Don't. You don't need to apologize to him."

I was floored. "Really?!" He nodded. "This coming from a man whose lips are tattooed on Mr. Robinson's ass?"

He shook his head while grinning. "Yeah, well, he'll live.

Plus, he's lucky if our kids call him uncle."

My heart fluttered. "God I love you!" I jumped on top of him, wrapped my arms around him, and kissed him, hard. *There's the man I married!*

However, before we went any further, he stopped me and said, "Hold on one second, babe." He lifted himself up.

I got off him, confused. "What's wrong?"

"Oh, nothing. I just have some presents for you," he replied, grabbing the bag.

I beamed. "Presents?"

"Yup."

He first pulled out a bouquet of fake flowers. My heart leapt; they were so gorgeous. "You went to our favorite florist?"

He nodded. "I simply told her I messed up and she created this beautiful bouquet. She said, 'She'll definitely forgive you with these.'"

"And she's not wrong." I replied, smelling them. She likes to spray her fake flowers with a scented mist and this time she did lavender. She knows how much I *love* lavender. I sank deep into the couch while taking in the wonderful fragrance.

"Awesome! But wait, there's more."

I sat back up and placed the flowers behind me on the couch. He then pulled out a box of chocolates from my favorite chocolatier. I melted. "Babe!"

"And there's only milk chocolates in there filled with either caramel, strawberry cream, or butter cream."

Tears started welling up in my eyes. "How did I get so lucky?" I asked, placing my hand on his cheek and caressing his face. He closed his eyes and gently rubbed his cheek into my hand.

Even though I didn't want to take my hand away, I *really* wanted one of the chocolates. "Sorry, babe." I dropped my hand, so I could open the box. I grabbed one and stuffed it into my mouth. My eyes rolled into the back of my head. "Oh, good Lord, why are these so good?!"

He chuckled. "And there's one more thing."

I sat up as I swallowed my heavenly morsel, almost choking on it. "There's more?"

He pulled out a small, square box that I recognized. I looked at him coyly. "Why do I have a funny feeling this is more for you than for me?"

He looked at me with lustful eyes. "Why not treat myself? I mean, we need to have some amazing makeup sex now, right?"

I let out a breathy laugh. "Yeah, you're right on that." I opened it and this beautiful, black lace babydoll lay in it. I glanced up at him and gave a sexy half smile. "I'm putting this on now!"

He put his hands up. "Please, don't let me stop you."

I ran to the bathroom to put it on. It was perfect. I thought, "How do I tell him not to rip it off immediately? I'm so in love with this!"

I walked out and his jaw dropped, like in the cartoons when they see a beautiful woman. I asked, "You like it?"

"No, baby, I love it! You look amazing!"

I blushed.

He crooked his finger at me. "Come here."

I walked over to him, climbed on top, and well … I think you can figure out what happened next.

JANUARY 6th

This morning, we drove home. It took us about six hours—since we made a couple of stops—but once we dropped off our luggage at our house, Jack stayed home to rest while I went out to run some errands. I don't know why it took me so long to do this, but I'm *finally* sending the boys a cell phone, so we can stay in touch. I guess because I felt they were fine and safe before but now, with everything going on, I'm worried and I want to know they're okay. Or maybe because I didn't want to (as Glen would say) "baby" them. But whatever the reason, waiting until May or June was not going to be an option. It would literally drive me insane.

During the drive, I told Jack what I wanted to do, since I wanted to add their phone onto our account. He agreed it was a good idea. "It's the best thing you can do right now. But how are you going to get it to them?"

"Oh, don't worry. I have an idea," I replied.

I walked into a local mobile store and was, of course, bombarded. "Hi! How are you? How can we help you today?"

Normally, I would think, "Can I please walk in and look before you attack me like I'm your next meal?" But this time I actually needed their immediate help. "I'm doing well, thank you. I'm actually in need of a new phone. Well, my brother is."

The youngest salesman walked around the counter and

said, "Oh, absolutely. Is there a particular brand you're looking to get him?"

Either it's your turn in the rotation or you're just being extremely ambitious! "Anything with a big keypad. He has big, fat fingers."

The salesman laughed. "Let me guess, you're the older sister."

I was a little surprised when he said that. "Yes, how did you know?"

"Because I have a little sister and I tease her all the time."

"Oh, okay, so you feel my pain."

We both laughed. He answered, "Yes, I do. But we also do anything and everything for them, right?"

"Exactly, like getting them a new phone."

"Absolutely. May I ask what happened to his old one?"

Here we go! "He dropped it and broke it. And he lives in a remote part of Washington, so it's hard for him to go into town and get a new one. Figured I would help him out."

Yeah, I got pretty good at spinning tales about my boys. It's not like I'm telling a complete lie, just partial truth mixed in with partial lies. I had to when *everybody* started asking me about them.

"Aw, you really are a nice sister."

I shrugged. "I try."

He brought me over to a display of tablets. "Now, I know you're probably wondering why I'm showing you our tablets instead of the phones." I nodded. "It's because the tablet can do pretty much everything a phone does, but is bigger, so this is beneficial to anyone with bad vision or, as you say, 'big, fat fingers.'"

I was impressed. "You know, I totally didn't think of

20

that."

He smiled smugly. "Not a lot of people do because they think a tablet is like a laptop, but it can do messages, calls, and video calls, like a phone."

As he explained and showed me all the different features, I knew this would be the right thing for them. Once he finished his spiel, I said, "Oh, perfect. I think they're going to love it."

"They?"

God damnit, Ashlynn! It took me a second before I answered, "Yeah, my brother and his partner."

"Oh, they'll be sharing?"

"Yeah. His partner isn't a big fan of phones, but understands he may need them in emergencies, so they just share one."

"Oh, okay. Makes sense." *Holy shit he bought it!* "I have relatives who live in the wilderness of Alaska and absolutely despise phones."

"So they must *love* you then."

For some reason, like it was a big secret, he leaned in and whispered, "They don't know I sell phones for a living."

We both roared with laughter. Once we composed ourselves, he asked, "Now, do either of you already have an account with us?"

"I do, but it's under my husband. Is that okay?"

That's where the "fun" ended; he became serious. "Um, are you adding a line to his account or opening a separate one for your brother?"

"Adding."

He made a face. "I'm sorry, but we do need his permission in order to do so."

"Not a problem. Is it okay if I call him and he gives the okay over the phone?"

He brightened up. "Oh, absolutely."

I whipped out my phone and called my love. I told him the situation and passed the phone over to the salesman, which I learned his name was Ryan. He asked Jack a few questions to confirm it was him and then the all-important, "Is it okay to add a line onto your account?"

I'm guessing Jack said yes because Ryan then said, "Okay, Mr. Graives, just wanted to make sure. Thank you very much for your confirmation."

He handed me back my phone and I said to Jack, "Thanks, babe."

"You're welcome, baby. I guess I'll see you soon?"

"Yeah, probably within the next hour or two."

"Sounds good. Love you."

"Love you, too."

We hung up. Ryan said, "Okay, Ashlynn, let's get everything set up for you."

"Great, thank you so much for your help, Ryan. And please forgive me for not getting your name earlier."

He chuckled. "Oh, it's fine. We got caught up in discussing our little siblings."

I tittered. "True."

About a half hour or so later, I walked out with a new tablet to send to my boys. I then went to the closest shipping center. Once again, I walked in to, "Hi, how can I help you today?"

Strolling over to the counter, I answered, "I have a rather odd request to make."

The gentleman behind the counter got a little

apprehensive. "Okay."

"I want to mail out this tablet to my brother, but he may not be home. He may be hiking in the woods, and I want to make sure he doesn't miss it, so I was hoping the driver could leave notes around the cabin to check his front door."

The guy relaxed a bit. "Oh, yeah, that's not a problem. Do you have the notes?"

"No, I was going to write them out here, if that's okay."

"Sure, do that while I get this packaged up for you."

"Thank you so much!" And that's exactly what I did. I wrote four notes to be placed on each side of the cabin. Three of them read, "Kaden, please check the front door. There's a package for you," while the one that was going on the front door read, "Kaden, this is for you. Please open ASAP," with an arrow pointing down. No offense to my brother, I love him dearly, but I trust Kaden more with this. And Roman … yeah, we won't even go there.

I handed the notes over to the guy. He grabbed an envelope and said, "I'm going to put the notes in this, tape it to the package, and write on it 'Driver, open when delivering and place around the cabin!' Hopefully, they won't ignore it."

"Awesome! Thank you again! I truly appreciate it!"

I paid and left, hoping and praying the driver would do their job. I also prayed Kaden, Roman, or Glen would find the package and I would hear from them soon.

JANUARY 13th

Finally, I heard from my boys today. It only took them a freaking week to find it! Geez!

Jack, the crew, and I were in the middle of packing things up, preparing for our long journey around the world for season three, when my phone rang. It was a video call from "My Boys <3." I made sure to punch in the new number to their tablet-phone thing immediately into mine, so I knew it was them when they called. I yelped and jumped for joy. "It's them!"

Jack smiled and said, "Go 'head and answer it, babe. We'll be fine."

I beamed, kissed him, and went into a different room to talk to my brothers. As I went to hit the "Answer" button, I hesitated for a quick second. I thought, "What if it isn't one of my boys? What if it's Nash, or someone else, or this Cillian character they told me about? What if some random person picked it up and is pulling a prank?" But that hesitation quickly dissipated. I only let it ring one more time before answering. Of course, it took the video feed a second to come up, but once it did, I saw my handsome boys. They shouted, "ALL FOR YOU ONE!"

Holy shit, our group motto! I almost forgot about it!

I glowed and screamed, "FUCK YOU, I AIN'T SHAR-ING!" We all laughed. "Oh my gosh, you guys have *no* idea how happy I am to see you!"

"We're happy to see you, too, sweetie," Kaden replied, holding the tablet, trying to get all of them in the shot.

"How are you guys doing? Are you okay?"

"Yeah, we're fine. Keeping out of trouble. Well, at least Glen and I are."

Roman retorted, "Hey, that asshole asked for it."

I shook my head and rubbed my forehead. "Oh, Roman. What did you do now?"

"Some guy was snooping around the cabin, so I scared him away. This is my home, bitch."

We all laughed again. "You haven't changed one bit, my friend."

He smiled. "Admit it, you miss me, baby."

I rolled my eyes and sighed. "Only a little." Kaden, Glen, and I roared with laughter while Roman didn't look amused. "I'm kidding. Of course, I miss you, you pain in the ass."

We all laughed some more before Kaden asked, "How are you doing, hon? How's the show coming along?"

"It's doing really well. We're number one in the network, which is huge."

They hooted and hollered. "That's awesome, hon."

"Congratulations, Ash."

"It's because of us, right? We truly made the show."

"Really, Roman?!" I shouted. "That's the first thing you think of?"

"Hey, that's huge and congratulations and all, but admit it, it's because of us."

I know I shouldn't have been, because it's fucking Roman, but I was shocked, pissed, and hurt.

Before I could respond, Glen yelled, "Dude, stop being

such a dick!"

"I'm not! I'm just saying!"

Kaden said, "Sorry, hon."

I answered, "No, it's okay. You guys don't know how badly I was against releasing that episode."

They were stunned. "Really?!"

Roman asked, "Why, Ash? I mean, I don't mind showing off this new physique of mine." He started posing like he was in a body building competition.

I shook my head again and chuckled. "I can't with you, Roman." Then I explained, "Because I felt like we were exploiting you guys for our benefit."

They all said in unison, "Aw, Ash."

Kaden tried to reassure me. "That's not the case at all."

Roman, on the other hand, didn't. "No, that is the case."

Glen and Kaden roared, "Roman!"

"What?! I'm just saying the truth! And it doesn't bother me at all, babe. Exploit me all you want."

I palmed my forehead. Kaden said, "Roman, just go away. Go over there, please," pointing to what I'm guessing was the woods.

He sulked and began walking away. "Sorry, Ash. Love you."

"Love you, too, jackass."

Then Kaden looked at Glen. "I'm sorry, bud, but can you give us a few?"

Glen became upset. "But, I want to talk to my sister."

Kaden placed his hand on Glen's shoulder. "And you will. I just need to talk to her first, okay?"

Glen looked at me. I nodded. "It's okay, Glen. We'll catch up in a bit."

It took a moment, but with a hint of pain in his voice, he responded "Fine," and walked away.

With Roman and Glen moving out of view, I could see the white snow all around them. "Oh my gosh, when did it snow?"

Kaden looked at me as if I lost my mind. "Honey, it's the middle of winter in Washington state. When isn't it snowing?"

I became concerned. "Oh, shit. Was the tablet damaged at all?"

"Obviously not, if we're using it."

I thought for a second. "Oh, yeah, duh!" I rubbed my forehead so hard I thought I was about to rip some skin off.

"Wow, Ash! Blonde moment much?!"

I glared at him. "Shut up, Kaden!"

We both laughed. He told me, "No, the delivery man must've wrapped the box in plastic and bubble wrap to make sure it didn't wet or damaged. There wasn't too much snow on it, though, when we found it."

I relaxed. "Oh, thank God. And I'm so glad they did that. Totally using that service from now on."

"Yeah, once we saw the signs, which, by the way, was freaking brilliant …"

I gave him a cheesy smile like a kid taking a picture. "Thanks!"

"Yeah, that was really smart actually since we're checking out the cabin at least once a week to make sure nobody is messing with it."

"Oh, awesome! Thank you! Mom and Dad would really appreciate that."

"Of course! So, again, after seeing the signs, we grabbed it and brought it inside, where we charged it. And here we are."

I waved my free arm around. "Yay! I'm so glad my plan worked!"

He laughed. "Which brings me back to why I want to talk to you. You sure everything is okay, hon? I mean, not to sound ungrateful, but out of the blue you send us this tablet when we haven't communicated in some time." My heart broke. He saw the pain in my face. "Aw, sweetie, I'm sorry. I didn't mean to upset you. But why did you send us this tablet? What's wrong?"

I took in a deep breath, let it out, and said, "I've been reading how …" I didn't want to call them monsters, so I tried my hardest to choose my words wisely, "… beings have been seen around Lake Minnetaha, Nonoma, and surrounding towns, destroying property and frightening locals and tourists. I was fearing either something happened to you guys or …"

"We were the ones causing the chaos."

I hesitated. "Yeah."

"I mean Roman I could see, but Glen and me? Really, Ash?"

"No, no, no! I know you and Glen would never, but I was fearing whatever serum you guys were injected with was messing with your minds."

"Oh, okay, that makes sense. I'll admit that's a constant fear I have, too, hon. That one day, I'm going to wake up and not be who I am because of this crap."

I started tearing up. "I'm so sorry, bud. If I could take this all back …"

"No, Ash. Don't say that. Don't blame yourself for any of this. We told you that when we reunited, and we'll continue to tell you that."

I heard Roman in the background, "Is she still blaming herself for this?"

"Yup!"

"Oh, tell her to stop!"

I laughed. I know it's not completely my fault, but every time I look into their, now, red eyes and see their dark, bark-like skin, my heart drops and I can't help but blame myself. If I didn't insist on them meeting the former sheriff, Mr. Mac-Reedy, then they still may have their beautiful brown eyes and handsome, smooth skin. Kaden said, "Seriously, sweetie, stop blaming yourself. If we didn't come here, we wouldn't have seen this beautiful area and I wouldn't have met Charlie."

I smiled. "This is true."

"And thankfully we're all fine. We've been staying pretty much in the same area, the valley behind the cabin. And like I said before, we keep an eye on it to make sure no one is trying to break in or destroy it. Like Roman said, 'It's our home, too.'"

Then we both said in unison, "Bitch," and laughed.

"So, I guess I'm reading about the others you broke out with?" I inquired.

"Oh, yes. I can guarantee it's Cillian and his goons. They thrive on fear and destruction."

"Oh, goodie. I hope we don't run into them when we come."

Kaden's eyes widened. "Wait, you're coming here? When?"

"Probably sometime in May or June."

A look of worry cascaded onto his face. "Ashlynn, I love you dearly and I would love nothing more than to see you, but please don't come here. It's not safe."

"Ha! Like that's stopped me before."

"No, seriously, Ash. Cillian, the guy we've told you about, is a *really* bad dude. If he gets a hold of you, we may not be able to protect you."

My heart skipped a beat. I felt concern–which means Kaden saw it–rush through me. I probably should've left it at that, but … this is me. I'm stubborn. And when I put my mind to something, I see it to the bitter end. I instantly regained my composure and said, "I don't care. I want to see you guys."

Kaden sighed. "I know you all too well, Ash, and I know this is one fight I won't win. We'll protect you the best we can when you get here."

I stood up a little taller, like I won this incredible debate, and gave him a half smile. "Thank you."

We conversed for a little bit longer before I talked to my brother and ended the video chat. As we hung up, we all made a promise to stay in contact via texting, calling, or video chat. And even though he would never do this, I teased Roman when I said, "You send me one dick pic and I will make sure to cut it off when I get there."

"Oh, baby! What did I tell you about that dirty talk?"

I laughed, "Seriously, Roman. One and gone."

He sighed. "Fine. You take all the fun away."

We all laughed and said our goodbyes.

It felt so good to finally see them and know that they're well and safe. But something within me was screaming that I should heed Kaden's warning and not go.

MAY 19th

It's been months but shooting finally wrapped for *Searching for the Truth*. As of yesterday, we were officially home and it's now time to compile all of the footage and sound recordings we have and make it into an eight-episode season. Thankfully, I don't have to worry about that, but I have been driving Jack crazy since we got home. The second we stepped foot in Sacramento, I turned to him and said, "Okay, when are we leaving for Lake Minnetaha?"

He looked at me. "Babe, we literally just got back, and we've got to get the episodes all set. But I promise you, once they are, we will be heading out."

I whined, "But that could take weeks."

"Baby, if I could make the process go faster, I would. But unfortunately, that's out of my control."

I sighed and grumbled in annoyance.

I have been staying in touch with my boys, though, these past few months. I've mainly been talking to Kaden, but Roman and I actually started our own weekly text. One day he sent me a silly selfie saying, "Admit it, you miss this face!"

It made me laugh out loud, which was kind of bad since Jack was in the middle of an interview. I apologized and excused myself. I first replied with, "You ass, you just got me in trouble with Jack for laughing during his interview." But then I took a hideous picture of myself and sent it, saying, "Admit it, you miss THIS face!"

From there, we started going back and forth with the selfies and we've been having so much fun with it. I'm just so relieved to know that they're still safe, that they're still fine. However, they told me that the others (meaning Cillian and his crew) have been out and about from the noises (screams) they've been hearing.

This morning, as the crew went to work on the episodes, I took it upon myself to start doing some research for our trip back. I may know everything, but I have to act like I know nothing, so I decided to call the newly appointed sheriff of Amitola Township to see if he had any "new" information for me. His name is Mark O'Neill. According to the guys, he's young—probably around our age, maybe a few years older—and, from what Kaden said, very handsome. I asked him one day, "Is he more handsome than Charlie?"

"Oh, no, Charlie is just as handsome." He paused for a moment.

I teased, "Why do I feel a 'but' coming up?"

"But I've always wanted to date a cop."

After dialing the sheriff's number, the line rang a couple of times before a woman answered. "Sheriff's office."

I was a little stunned. Usually, Mr. MacReedy answered the phone. There was never any secretary or anything like that. "Hi, yes, I was wondering if Sheriff O'Neill is available."

"He's not, he's busy on the other line. May I take a message?"

"Yes, please. My name is Ashlynn Graives and I was hoping …"

"Yes, Mrs. Graives, he's been expecting you," she interjected.

"Expecting me?" I questioned, shocked.

"Yes, give me the best number for you and I'll see that he calls you back immediately."

"Okay ..." I gave her my number and that was that.

"He's expecting me?" I thought. "I don't know if I should be honored or frightened."

About fifteen minutes later, he called me back. "Sheriff O'Neill, it's a pleasure."

"Pleasure is all mine, Mrs. Graives. How can I help you?"

It was kind of weird not hearing a strong Texas accent come through the line. His voice was not as brash; it was ... lighter, if that makes any sense. At the same time, though, it was refreshing. "So, I have a show called *Searching* ..."

"*Searching for the Truth*. I know all about it, Mrs. Graives, and I must say, I'm a fan."

I grinned from ear to ear. I have to admit, it's *so* cool when someone recognizes the title of a show you're working on and says they're a fan. "Thank you, that's kind of you to say. And, please, call me Ash ..."

"And let me guess, you would like some information about our monster infestation."

My smile disappeared. "Yes, I was hoping ..."

"Mrs. Graives, I know about you and your history with the previous sheriff, Mr. MacReedy. I also know it's because of your show that our quiet, little, tourist township became a hotbed for novice investigators and filmmakers to come in and try to find these creatures."

Shit! I rolled my eyes, not in disgust or annoyance, but because I knew he was right, and in all technicality, we fucked up. The boys have been telling me how they've seen and heard people walking around in the woods, trying to find them, meaning the creatures. We turned a place I called my home into Disneyland for thrill seekers, paranormal enthusiasts, and anyone looking to be the next Jack Graives. I apologized profusely. "Sheriff, if there's anything I can do …"

"I would love to tell you to never come back to this area, Mrs. Graives, but I'm not that type of person, nor do I truly have the authority to do that." I let out a breath of relief. "However, I will tell you this; watch the videos that are online of what's been happening in this area. Watch them and then let me know if you still want to come back. Maybe we'll talk more then."

I nodded my head. "I will, Sheriff. Thank you very much for your …" Before I could finish, he hung up.

I placed my phone down and buried my face in my hands. "Well, that went well."

After a moment or two of kind of collecting myself, I did as the sheriff told me. I looked online and there were a good thirty videos I was able to find … and I watched them all. I was in utter shock as I did, seeing what the creatures were doing: destroying public property, scaring people, etc.

However, there was one video that chilled me to my core. It was a group of guys–a normal group, not these damn thrill seekers looking to "interact" with them–walking through the woods when they came across a creature. But this one wasn't "ordinary," this one was massive. He was a good two or three feet taller than my boys and they were already standing at over six feet. When I saw him, I said, "That must be Cillian."

My skin crawled, my hair stood on end, and a chill went up and down my spine.

My boys weren't kidding. I thought, "Hopefully, we don't run into him when we go back."

MAY 20th

I decided to wait before calling back Sheriff O'Neill. Figured I would give him some time to "cool down." This time, when I asked for the sheriff, his secretary said, "Give me one moment, Mrs. Graives. He's been expecting you."

Yay …

I was only on hold for a couple of seconds before the sheriff came on the line. In a cheerful voice, he said, "Good morning, Mrs. Graives. It's a pleasure to hear from you."

I was absolutely flabbergasted. I actually took the phone away from my ear for a second to make sure I dialed the right number. I honestly thought he was going to re-rip me a new one. I responded, somewhat puzzled, "Yes, sir, it's nice to talk to you, too."

He chuckled. "I know my tone has caught you off guard …" *You think!* "… but I must apologize for my actions yesterday; they were absolutely uncalled for." I listened, my mouth agape. "You must understand where I'm coming from, though. I'm from this area. I was born in Seattle, but I was raised in Thunderbird, the next town over from Nonoma. This is truly my home. After I went away to college and the police academy, I came home to monsters destroying it and people running amok. And then I heard the previous sheriff just up and left. Well after that, let's just say I wasn't too happy."

"That's understandable, sir."

"But the truth is, it wasn't just your episode that started the craze. Things got worse once the news media started printing articles and posting videos of them."

I joked, trying to lighten the mood, "Damn media! Always making things worse and causing chaos!"

Sheriff O'Neill roared with laughter. "Exactly. But my point is, I shouldn't have been so rude to you and I'm truly sorry."

"Thank you, Sheriff. Apology accepted."

He paused for a moment. "So, I'm guessing the reason you called in the first place was to ask me some questions about these things."

"Yes, if you don't mind and if you have the time."

"I'm all ears. Ask away and I will answer to the best of my abilities. Will this be used in the show?"

"Only if you give me the okay."

"You have my permission."

"Great, just give me one second." I put him on speaker and started my recorder. "So, the main question I have for you, Sheriff, is do you know what these things could be?"

He replied, "Honestly, I think they're burned up Bigfeet from the raging forest fires that hit the West Coast not too long ago. I mean, that's what they look like to me."

"Could it be possible that these things are ..." *Don't say it, Ashlynn, don't say it!* "That they're medical experiments gone wrong?"

"Hm ... never thought of that. Like they're human beings that have been badly deformed?"

"Yes, sir."

"Well, I guess anything is possible. But we don't live in

the movies, Mrs. Graives."

Oh, if only you knew!

I chuckled. "No, we don't, sir. So, why that area? Why do you think Amitola Township and its surrounding areas are being so affected by these creatures?"

"Mrs. Graives, I've been asking myself those questions every single day."

June 15th

I did not sleep at all. Between being so excited to see my boys again and nervous about what we might find, I couldn't. You could've given me melatonin and/or a sleeping pill and I still wouldn't have gone to bed!

When Jack woke up around 4 a.m. to get ready, he found me sitting on the couch in our living room watching TV. Groggily, he asked, "Hey, baby. You okay?"

I looked over my shoulder and responded, "Yeah, why?"

"Because it's four in the morning."

My eyes widened. "Holy shit! Are you serious?" He nodded. "Damn. I thought it was like midnight or something."

He came over and sat next to me. "Excited to see the guys?"

"What do you think?" I answered, chuckling. "But I'm also a little nervous, borderline scared, at what we might find. Will any Black Op groups be there? Will this Cillian guy or any other creatures show up? For the first time ever since my parents got that cabin, I'm actually a little hesitant about going."

He rubbed my back. "Don't worry, babe. It'll all be fine. Let me go shower and get ready and then we'll head to the airport. You want to call the crew to make sure they're up and then join me in the shower? I can help you take your mind off things for a little bit." He leaned in and nuzzled my neck.

I giggled. "Well, it's a good thing we have two hours before we have to be at the airport."

"Oh, yeah!" Jack picked me up, threw me over his shoulder like a barbarian, and carried me to the bathroom as I laughed and screamed.

Ah, the crew can sleep for another hour, it's fine!

We got to the airport a little after six and our flight left around eight. By ten we were in Seattle and about a half hour later we were on our way to the cabin. That's when the sandman decided to hit me. All I remember was resting my head against the back driver-side window as we got onto the highway and that's about it. I have no clue how long I was asleep for, but I was literally shaken awake by a sizable vibration. I yawned and stretched from my seated position. My eyes slowly opened, and I looked around. I was alone in our rental car. I guess they didn't want to disturb me, or they tried waking me and I wasn't budging. They probably figured the boys weren't too far, so I would be safe. And I'm sure Jack checked on me often.

However, as the sands left my eyes and my vision cleared, I noticed something strange: something was staring at me from in front of the car. My sight immediately focused, and I jumped a little. Whoever or whatever it was, it definitely wasn't one of my boys. It may have had the same fire red eyes and burnt-looking skin, like them, but it was gigantic in size. It was literally bending down with its hands on its knees in order to look at me. Now, mind you, we were renting a 2001 Jeep Grand Cherokee and this thing was … I don't even know, but it was definitely taller than it and almost as wide. Yeah, this dude was *huge!*

Seconds later, I realized who it was, and my heart skipped a beat. "Cillian." He smirked. "Shit!"

He stood up straight and walked around to where I was

sitting. He went to open the door, but I immediately locked it and the driver's door, as well. As he slowly went around to the front passenger door, I jumped up and locked it just in time as well as that side's back door. He growled. He went to the back-passenger side door, bent down, and in a gravelly voice said, "You think doing all of that will stop me from getting in."

Before I could answer, he stood up, balled his fist, wound up, and punched through the glass like it was water. I screamed, trying to cover myself, but I still got cut up pretty good from the flying shards. I touched where I felt stinging pain–mainly my cheeks and near my mouth–and found blood. Even my forearms were bleeding. That's when I heard the front door of the cabin open and Jack yelling, "Ashlynn!"

Jack and the crew came out, but immediately stopped in their tracks when they saw Cillian. The monster bellowed, "Don't take one step closer!"

I yelled from the car, "Listen to him, Jack!" I figured out *very* quickly this Cillian was no joke. I didn't want anything to happen to my husband or my friends.

Jack nodded, but his eyes screamed with so much concern and fear. Mine did, too, but they also begged him to stay safe. Cillian then walked back to the front of the car. I went to the middle, thinking he was coming to the other side, but he stopped and proceeded to pick up the front, so we could be eye-to-eye. He lifted it up like it was a fucking feather. The bastard smiled at me with so much pride and said, "Impressed?"

My heart was beating faster than a thoroughbred in a race, and I was scared out of my mind, but I sternly replied, "Not in the least!"

His smirk left his face and he growled. "Then, I guess I need to try harder. You might want to put a seatbelt on."

Without thinking twice, I found it and put it on.

He continued pushing the car up until it was straight, pointing right at the sky. I was screaming while my arms were pushing on the roof and my feet were on the center console to hold myself in place. I knew Jack and the crew couldn't do anything. They stood there helplessly, yelling at Cillian to put me down. However, I was also hoping my boys weren't too far away to save me. Cillian laughed. "You know what they say, 'What goes up must come down.'"

He let go of the car and slightly pushed it, so it would fall backwards. "JACK!"

Before the car completely fell, I felt it stop abruptly. "We got you, Ash!"

I contorted my neck to look out the rearview window and saw two sets of abnormal feet. I let out a massive breath. "Oh, thank God!"

In the distance, I heard fighting and roars. "You better stay away from her, Cillian!"

He cackled. "Or what will you do against me, Kaden? I'm a fucking god compared to you! I will be back!"

Then I heard–and felt–heavy footsteps running away. Seconds later, I heard, "You okay, hon?"

"Yeah, but I think I would be a little bit better if I was right side up! You know, the whole blood rushing to the head thing!"

"Oh, shit! Of course! Hold on one second!"

Slowly, and carefully, they brought the car to the right position. I sat in it, breathing heavily, waiting for the blood to pour back into my body as everyone rushed over to me.

Kaden was right next to the window that Cillian punched out. He reached his hand in and caressed my head, "You sure you're okay, hon?"

I was about to answer him when I heard the door handle on the other side being violently tugged at. I looked over to see Jack trying to open it. I unlocked it and he jumped in. He threw his arms around me and held me tight–a little too tight. "Oh my gosh, baby, are you okay?"

His shoulder was digging into my neck. I patted his back and wheezed, "Jack."

"Yeah, baby?"

Gasping for air, I replied, "You're choking me."

"Oh, shit! Sorry, hon!" He let go and I coughed as I caught my breath.

After bringing me inside, Roman, Kaden, and Glen stood around in the living room, watching for anything, while I sat on the couch so Jerry could patch me up. "You're lucky none of these cuts are deep, Ash," he said, dabbing a swab filled with peroxide on the cuts on my face.

"Dude, I'm lucky I made it out of there alive!"

Jerry nodded. "True"

Roman chimed in, "We told you, Ash. Cillian is no joke."

"But how the hell is he so much bigger and stronger than you guys?"

All three of my boys cried out, "Woah, hey, who said anything about being stronger than us?"

"Seriously, he just picked up a goddamn Jeep like it was a piece of paper!" The three of them went silent. "Yeah, that's what I thought."

Then Roman started in, "Well, I once picked up …"

Everybody–from Jack to Chad to Greg to Jerry and of

course Glen, Kaden, and I–yelled, "Shut up, Roman!"

I added, "This is *so* not the time!"

He mumbled, "Just saying."

As Jerry finished up with my wounds, Glen exclaimed, "Uh, guys!"

We looked at him. A laser point was directed at his chest. He looked at us. "I don't think we're alone."

That's when there was a knock at the door. I got up and walked over to it. Before I opened it, I looked over at Greg and whisper-shouted, "Are the cameras up and running?"

He nodded. "We got them up while you were asleep."

Damn! I really must've been out for some time!

I took a deep breath and opened the door. Standing in front of me was a tall (maybe 6' 1") and somewhat bulky man in a military uniform. His legs were spread shoulder-width apart and his hands were folded behind him. At his back stood several other military men wielding their guns. The guy in front of me, who I presumed was the "leader" of the operation, asked in a very stern and authoritative voice, "Are you Mrs. Ashlynn Graives?"

Oh, crap! "Yes."

"My name is Sergeant Major William O'Hare. May we come in?"

I stood up straighter and answered, "Yes, as long as your men put down their weapons, including the one that is aimed at my brother."

"Yes, ma'am." He raised up a balled fist and they instantly lowered their guns.

Holy shit!

I looked over at Glen and there was no longer a red point on him. I turned back to the sergeant major and his team, and

43

said, "Please," as I motioned them in. They filed in one by one. They all stood by me until everyone was in. I watched them enter, mesmerized at how many there were. I whispered, "Like a fucking clown car."

"What was that?" Sergeant Major asked.

My heart leapt into my throat, like I got caught saying something bad in front of my parents. "Nothing." The last one walked in, and I closed the door. "Please, follow me."

I led them into the living room. I went and sat next to Jack on the couch while the sergeant major sat in the armchair across from us. His goons stood behind him while my boys and Jack's crew stood behind us.

Sergeant Major O'Hare stated, "We have a common enemy, Mrs. Graives."

"Cillian," I replied in a straight voice.

"Yes, ma'am. They shouldn't be alive either," looking at and pointing to Roman, Kaden, and Glen.

I seethed, "They're not the true enemy here, Sergeant Major. Plus, you harm them, and we will expose you."

He glared at me. "What do you mean expose us? You have nothing on us, Mrs. Graives."

"Wanna bet?" I replied, crossing my arms. "We went to the lab and taped what was in there, or at least what was left after the carnage."

"You're bluffing."

I raised an eyebrow. "Try me."

We stared each other down for a good couple of seconds. Then Jack added, "Also, Sergeant Major, we have cameras up around the cabin, both inside and out." The sergeant major looked around. "So all of this is being recorded, as well."

I remarked, "You may want to be careful what you say,

sir."

Roman just had to put his two cents in. "You just got burned, dick."

Glen and Kaden smacked him while I growled, through gritted teeth, "Roman, shut it!"

The sergeant major stared at me for another moment or two, sizing me up. "What are you proposing, Mrs. Graives?"

I smirked. "We work together to take out Cillian and whoever else is destroying this area. Once that's done, you leave them," pointing to my boys, "alone and let them live in peace."

Sergeant Major shook his head. "I don't think we can come to that agreement, Mrs. Graives."

I was ruffled. "Why?"

"Because they," again, pointing to my boys, "have been causing chaos and destruction in this area, as well."

Roman yelled out, "Bullshit," as he took a step toward them.

Jack and I stood up as we all held him back. Then Sergeant Major's team raised their weapons, pointing them at Roman. I raised my hand up in front of me. "Woah, woah! Please, Sergeant Major, call off your men."

He stood up, turned around, and shouted, "Did I give an order to raise your guns?!"

They all shouted back in unison, "No, sir!"

"Then put those goddamn things down!"

Immediately, they rested their weapons once again. Sergeant Major turned back to us. "My apologies, Mrs. Graives."

I nodded. My heart was racing, and I was breathing a little heavy. "It's okay. Roman is sorry, too." I looked at him. "Right, Roman?"

He snarled. I leaned in and said to him the one thing I knew he hated hearing, "I swear to God, I will make sure Mom disowns you if you don't cut your shit!"

He relaxed a little and said, "Sorry."

Everyone in the room started to calm down. Kaden then said, "Sergeant Major, I can swear on my life that we have not done anything wrong. We have not destroyed any property or any buildings ..."

"Since the lab," Sergeant Major cut in.

Kaden sighed. "Yes, since the lab. We can guarantee it's Cillian and his gang."

Sergeant Major thought for a moment. "There were fifteen of you who escaped. We've killed at least six."

"Which means Cillian could have at least five with him," Kaden answered.

Glen added, "But don't forget, one of them is Nash, who is dumber than a box of rocks."

Kaden reminded, "But is still very strong, which makes him more dangerous."

Sergeant Major continued thinking. *Oh, come on, man! This is not rocket science!* A few seconds later, he responded, "Okay, if you help us take them out, I swear we will leave you alone."

I ordered, "I want that in writing, Sergeant Major." He leered at me with scornful intent. "You should know, sir, to never make a verbal agreement. It may just come back and bite you in the ass."

Jack and the boys cackled behind me. Sergeant Major grinned; he seemed to be impressed. "Okay then. We will be back tomorrow with an agreement."

I walked over to him and held out my wrapped-up hand. "See you tomorrow, Sergeant Major O'Hare."

He gently grasped my hand and shook it. "See you tomorrow, Mrs. Graives."

We let go of each other's hands. That's when from behind him, I saw two glowing red eyes a few feet above him. My eyes widened. "Oh, shit! It's Cillian!" I exclaimed, pointing toward where I was seeing him.

Sergeant Major's troops turned, raised their guns, and started firing. I covered my head as Jack shielded me and then the boys protected us from any flying debris. Once their magazines ran out, they immediately switched them out. Cillian must've gotten away because I heard Sergeant Major scream, "Get after him," and a stampede of boots running out the door.

As they left, my boys stood up, which made Jack and me stand up. Glen said, "Let's go," but I grabbed him before he went anywhere.

"No, you guys need to stay here!"

"No, Ash, we need to go after Cillian," Roman replied.

"And be mistaken for an enemy and get shot by those trigger-happy morons? Yeah, I don't think so! Please stay here with us, with me." I grabbed his forearm, knowing that would have an effect on him.

He groaned. "Fine. But next time, I'm going after that son of a bitch."

I smiled. "Deal." That's when I panned over to the windows that looked out into the forest and really saw the damage. I gasped, placing my hands over my mouth. "Fuck! Mom and Dad are going to kill me!"

Glen came over, placed his hand on my shoulder, and said, "Yeah, have fun telling them …"

Before he could finish, I let my arms fall back down to

my sides, looked over my shoulder, and shouted, "Fuck off, Glen!"

He raised his arms and stepped away. Jack came over, wrapped his arm around my shoulders and said, "Don't worry about this, babe. We'll clean it up and get it all fixed. Your parents won't even know what happened."

I sulked. "Yeah, easy for you to say."

He asked, "Isn't your cousin, Mel, in home renovation?"

"Yeah, but he's all the way in New Jersey. And I'm not asking him to come out here, especially now."

"No, I'm not saying that. I'm saying once everything is cleared up here, ask him to come and fix this up. He can even bring Danielle and Kevin if he wants. Give them a nice little family vacation while he works on this."

I thought about it for a second. "That's not a terrible idea."

"You see. Now, why don't you get some rest. You've been through enough already."

I nodded, gave him a kiss, and went toward our room as he grabbed his crew to help him clean up. However, as I was about to go down the hallway, Kaden, Roman, and Glen stopped me. Kaden said, "You know, you haven't given us a proper hello yet."

I beamed, went over to him, and wrapped my arms tightly around him. He, of course, reciprocated. After letting him go, I did the same to Roman and my baby brother. "I missed you guys so much."

"We missed you, too," Glen said.

After letting go of Glen, Kaden asked, "Want some company?"

I answered, "It's not necessarily that I *want* some

company, it's that I *need* it."

We all laughed as they followed me into what was my bedroom and is now Jack and my room. We all talked and laughed, taking my mind off what had happened earlier, making me forget that a behemoth monster was lurking in our backyard.

JUNE 16th

At some ungodly hour, Jack and I were jolted awake by loud banging and cutting noises. "What the fuck was that?" I practically screamed.

Still half asleep, Jack said, "Stay here, I'll go see."

He got out of bed and stumbled out of the room. Seconds later, he came back in, more alert, and said, "Babe, you have to come and see this."

"See what?" I responded, beyond irritated.

"The soldiers are fixing up the living room."

"What?!"

I jumped out of bed and speed-walked toward the door to see what the hell he was talking about. Jack grabbed me before I headed out. I looked at him. "Let go of me, Jack!" I was in no mood to be stopped, even for some "fun" time.

"I'm not letting you go out there like that."

"Like what?!" That's when I looked down and realized I didn't put my robe on. I was just in shorts and a tank top with no bra. "Oh … fair enough."

I sprinted back into the room, put it on, and went out into the living room. I walked in to see our crew watching as a handful of soldiers worked on the windows and walls they destroyed yesterday. Chad looked at me. "Good morning, Ash."

"Good, no. Morning, yes."

"Uh oh, boys, step aside. She's on a rampage," he said to

Greg and Jerry, pushing them out of my way. They know I'm not a morning person *at all* and to be awakened by such loud noises is one of my biggest pet peeves in life.

One of the soldiers turned to me and said, "I'm sorry, Mrs. Graives, for the loud noises. We wanted to make amends for shooting out your living room walls and windows by fixing them."

I calmed down a little. "I appreciate that, soldier, but ..."

"My name is Sergeant Ramirez, ma'am."

I glared at him. "I appreciate what you're doing, Sergeant Ramirez, but it's ..." I looked around for the time.

"It's past oh seven hundred, ma'am."

"Oh seven hundred?"

"Sorry. It's past seven o'clock, ma'am. According to county ordinance, we can start working at this time."

Not realizing what time it was–thinking it was much earlier than that–I felt extremely foolish for running out, ready to start a war. I softened my stance and my facial expression. "I'm sorry, Sergeant. I ... I didn't know."

"It's okay, Mrs. Graives. We thought about waiting until you woke up and telling you, but we also felt obligated to repair all of this after what we did, so we just started working. Figured, 'It's easier to ask forgiveness than ...'"

I chimed in, saying the rest of the quote with him, "'... it is to get permission.'"

He smiled. "You know the quote?"

"Absolutely. Admiral Grace Hopper once said it."

"Yes, ma'am. So, do we have your forgiveness?"

I smiled. "And my permission."

"Thank you, Mrs. Graives."

"No, thank *you*, Sergeant. One less thing for me to worry

about now."

He chuckled. "My pleasure, ma'am."

He went back to work while I asked, "Who's hungry?"

The crew, of course, replied in unison, "Me!"

I tittered. "Figured that. Let me go get dressed and I'll get started on breakfast."

"Yes!" they all exclaimed.

I turned to head toward my room when I saw Jack standing there, staring at me. I wished I could say with lustful eyes, but I actually saw a hint of jealousy in them. I stared back at him and asked, "What?"

He shook his head. "Nothing," and stepped to the side to let me go by.

"Okay," I said, somewhat confused, as I walked past him.

I got dressed and cooked up some waffles. We, of course, offered food and drink to them, but they politely declined. They wanted to get more work done before taking any breaks.

A couple of hours later, Sergeant Major O'Hare returned to the cabin with a folder in his hand. "Mrs. Graives," he said in his stern, authoritative voice.

"Sergeant Major," I replied, sitting up straight.

He handed me the folder. "The agreement you asked for."

I relaxed my stance, shocked that he actually wrote up and brought me an agreement. I took it from him. "Oh. Thank you, Sergeant Major. I'll read through it and sign it."

"Very good. There are two copies: one is yours and one is ours. I already signed both."

I nodded. "Sounds good."

He then softened his voice. "And I also want to apologize for the damage done to your cabin last night. Sergeant

Ramirez is a great worker and will have it looking like new in no time."

"Thank you, Sergeant Major. I truly appreciate what you and your team are doing. And I can already tell that my parents won't even know what happened."

We looked over his shoulder to see Sergeant Ramirez and his team working hard on the windows, walls, and floors of the cabin. It was already looking like nothing had ever happened. Sergeant Major looked back at me, did a slight bow, and said, "Our pleasure, ma'am. If you have any questions while reading through the agreement, just let me know."

"Will do, sir."

As I began perusing through it, with Jack and Chad looking over my shoulders, we came across a paragraph stating, "Soldiers will be stationed outside and inside the cabin at all times for the protection of Mrs. Ashlynn Graives, her husband, Mr. Jack Graives, and their crew members."

"Oh, well ain't that just fucking dandy," I mumbled.

Jack whispered to me, "Babe, I know you're not a big fan of that, but I think that's going to be best. We'll be safe in here instead of wondering where the hell Cillian or any other creature is." I rolled my eyes, knowing he was right.

My boys and their protection throughout this whole thing were mentioned in the very beginning of the agreement and that's all that really mattered to me. We finished reading, I signed both copies, and handed one of them back to the sergeant major. He said, "I guess everything was to your liking, Mrs. Graives?"

I smiled and nodded. "I'm not exactly a big fan of you all being around the cabin at all times, but I understand it's for our protection and I appreciate that. Thank you for having your troops stay. I'll make sure they're taken care of with food and water."

"Thank you. I'm sure they'll appreciate that."

He turned to go do whatever he was working on while I went back to Jack and the crew. I had a funny feeling this was going to be a long trip.

****

Just before the sun set, Sergeant Ramirez and his team were done with the living room. It was amazing! You would've *never* thought that the wall facing the woods was just blown out by rifles. They did an immaculate job. I stared at the brand-new walls and windows, my mouth almost reaching the floor. Sergeant Ramirez walked up next to me and said, "I guess we did a good job?"

I looked at him. "Good? How about great? Amazing? Exceptional? Need I go on?"

He laughed. "No, I think I got it. Thank you for the kind words."

"No, thank you for doing this. How can I ever repay you?"

"Well, all of the food you cooked today looked and smelled amazing."

"And I did offer you some."

He tittered. "Yes, you did and thank you. I just didn't want to take a break when we were doing so well."

"Understandable. I do that a lot myself."

He looked at me with pleading eyes. "Are there any leftovers I could have?"

"Oh, absolutely! Follow me."

We went into the kitchen and I opened up the refrigerator. "What would you like?"

He stared at everything, on the verge of drooling. "Oh, gosh. Where do I begin?"

I laughed and blushed. It's nice to have people other than my husband, friends, and family gush over my food. I'm not a chef, per se, but I do love to cook! I asked, "What's your palette screaming for?"

"Oh, whatever you made for lunch smelled amazing and I've been craving that."

"Oh, the paninis? There's a ham one left and a turkey one. Would you like both?" I asked as I reached in for them.

His eyes widened like a kid at a candy store being told they can have whatever they want. "May I?"

I chortled. "Of course. Would you like them heated up?"

"Please. I haven't had a warm meal in God knows how long."

"Don't worry, Sergeant. I got you."

I went to warm up the paninis and then grabbed a plate, a napkin, and some utensils for him. "Please, sit," as I motioned to the dining room table.

"Thank you, Mrs. Graives."

"Please call me, Ashlynn."

He smiled. "Thank you, Ashlynn."

He sat at the dining room table and moments later, I met him there with the paninis. I was ready to offer the other soldiers who were with him some food and drink, but they went outside. Jerry went out for me to ask if they wanted anything, and they said no. *Well, when Sergeant Major asks me why his troops aren't eating or drinking, I will gladly tell him they told me no! Their freaking loss!*

He took a bite of the ham and melted in his chair. "Holy shit!" He looked at me, embarrassed. "I'm sorry, ma'am! I didn't mean to curse in front of you!"

I laughed out loud. "Oh, please! I curse like a fucking sailor! Let loose, my friend!"

He relaxed and let out a massive breath. "Oh, thank God. I was raised in a house where even if you said, 'Damn,' or 'Hell,' you were beaten until your backside was redder than a cooked lobster."

I rubbed my lower back, since I was sitting, feeling his pain. "Ouch! Yeah, I've been there!"

"You? I'm sure you were miss goody two shoes."

"HA! Yeah, even when my brother, Glen, did something wrong, I was blamed because I'm the older child and should set a good example for him."

He shrugged. "I'm the youngest and I have to agree."

I gasped in mock horror. "How dare you! No more paninis for you!"

I went to "take away" the plate when Sergeant Ramirez begged, "Please, no! This is so fucking good! Older siblings are always right!"

We both let out a bellowing laugh. After a moment, he continued to eat, and we continued to talk, learning more about each other. I even asked him why he's working for the Black Ops. He said, "It's a job, so I can care for my wife and daughter at home."

I had to ask, "Did you know what they were doing at the lab?"

His face became long and sunken. "Unfortunately, I did. I didn't agree with what they were doing, but there was nothing I could do. I'm sorry."

"Sergeant Ramirez, I'm not looking for an apology from you. I'm looking for one from the man who took them away from me."

"You mean Sheriff MacReedy?"

I nodded, feeling my face become hot and bright red from the anger welling up inside me and the tears I was trying to hold back.

Sergeant Ramirez asked, "Ashlynn, if you ever saw him again and he did apologize, would you even accept it?"

As I quickly wiped away any tears starting to roll down my cheeks, I sniffled and replied, "I honestly don't know. Every time I do think about that scenario possibly happening, I get so angry, and I just imagine myself beating him to his very last breath."

Sergeant Ramirez was startled by what I said. "I'm sorry, Ashlynn. I didn't mean to bring up such a sour subject for you."

I continued wiping away the tears and shook my head. "No, it's not your fault. I technically brought it up first."

Once Sergeant Ramirez finished his dinner, he thanked me for the food and was about to go to his tent when Greg came running over. "I just saw a creature on the screen."

We looked at him. I asked, "Where? Is it Roman, Kaden, or Glen?"

He shook his head. "I don't think so but come look."

"I'm going to grab Sergeant Major," Ramirez said as I followed Greg.

"Sounds good. Meet us in Greg's room."

"Copy."

We went into his room–which was Kaden's room–and over to his desk holding all of the screens. After hearing all of the commotion, Chad, Jerry, and Jack joined us. "What's going on?" Jack asked.

I looked at him. "Greg saw a creature on one of the cameras."

"Where?"

Greg answered, "The furthest camera out."

Seconds later, as Greg was pulling up the footage, Sergeant Major entered the room. "Where's the creature?"

Greg repeated, "I saw it on the camera that's furthest away from here."

"Which is?" Sergeant Major inquired.

"About a half mile that way," pointing with his left hand, "into the forest."

"Do we know who it is?" Sergeant Major asked.

I replied, "No, not yet. We're about to look and see."

Greg played the video, and we watched a creature scouting the area. I immediately knew, "That's not one of my boys."

"Then I'm gathering up my troops and heading out to see if we can find it and get it."

He turned and walked out of the room. I–along with Jack and the crew–followed him. "Wait, Sergeant Major." I grabbed my light jacket since it was a little chilly out.

The sergeant major looked at me. "What do you think you're doing?"

"I'm coming with you."

"The hell you are," Jack and Sergeant Major O'Hare hollered in unison.

"Holy shit, is there a fucking echo?!" I exclaimed as I slightly covered my ears. "Look, you guys don't understand. I'm the only one who can recognize my brothers from the others. I don't want anything to happen to them, obviously, so I'll come with you to let you know if it's them or not."

Jack argued, "You're not going, Ash," while Sergeant

Major asked, "How long will it take you to identify?"

"Seconds."

He thought for a moment. "Okay, fine, but *stay close!*"

I gave him a half smile. "Yes, sir."

He walked out the door. "All right, everyone, move out!"

As I was about to follow, Jack gently grabbed my arm. "Please, babe, don't do this. Stay here with me."

I reasoned, "Jack, if they shoot Glen or Roman or Kaden when I could've prevented it, I'll never forgive myself."

"Yeah, but … you know he's out there."

I looked down. "I know." Then I looked back up at him. "But you know I don't really sit around doing nothing."

He smiled, his eyes shining with so much love and understanding. That's when I said, grasping his hand, "Come with me and be my knight."

He was about to answer when Sergeant Ramirez came over. "I'm sorry, ma'am, but we're only taking one civilian with us and that's you. We shouldn't even be doing that, but you put up a good fight." A shit-eating grin came across my face. He looked at Jack. "I'll take good care of her, sir. I'll make sure she's safe."

I could see in Jack's eyes he wasn't too keen on this idea, but he eventually agreed. "Thank you, Sergeant. I appreciate that."

Wait a minute! Am I once again seeing a hint of jealousy in my man's eyes?

Sergeant Ramirez said, "My pleasure, sir." He panned over to me. "We better get going, Ashlynn."

"I'm right behind you."

He turned and walked away as I looked at my amazing husband. He said, "You come back to me."

I kissed him and placed my forehead on his. "I always do."

I kissed him one more time before walking away. Right before I went out the door, I turned back to him. "I love you."

"I love you, too."

I left, praying I was doing the right thing.

****

Sergeant Ramirez was waiting for me outside. "Ready, Ashlynn?"

"Yuppers. Let's go."

We started walking. His fellow soldiers were already a few yards ahead of us, so we double-timed our walk to catch up. As we did, he asked, "So how long have you and Mr. Graives been together?"

"Married or …?"

We started to slow down as we caught up. He replied, "Like together together."

"Oh, most of our lives."

He looked at me, eyes somewhat widened. "I'm sorry?"

I explained how Jack and I met. When I finished, he said, "Wow. That's beautiful."

I nodded. "Yeah, I sometimes can't believe I was *that* lucky."

That's when one of his fellow troopers turned toward us with daggers in his eyes and placed his index finger in front of his lips, telling us to be quiet. I mouthed, "Sorry."

He shook his head and turned back around. Sergeant Ramirez and I looked at each other and silently giggled like teenagers.

We kept on walking for a little while, stopping every so often to listen and look through the forest. It was getting dark, so visibility was getting low, but we kept on going.

Oh, yeah, this is a brilliant idea!

At one point, I looked back to see the cabin was barely visible. Then I heard, "Ash," being called out. It wasn't a normal "human" voice, but the gruffy voice I have become familiar with from my boys and the creatures. I looked around to realize I was alone. Somehow, during the search, I got away from the soldiers. Seriously, don't ask me how I pulled that off because I still don't have the faintest clue. I said to myself, "Shit! Nice job, Ash!"

I scanned the forest with my flashlight. "Glen?"

I saw nothing, but I heard again, "Ash, over here."

"Glen, is that you?"

I started walking toward the voice. *Yup, here we go! Another bad fucking idea, Ash!*

Thankfully, the full moon was coming in, so if my flashlight decided to die, I still had some sort of light. Of course, no sooner did I have that thought my freaking flashlight went out. "Oh, you've got be fucking kidding!"

Then I heard footsteps coming from all around me. "Glen! Roman! Kaden!" I was starting to panic.

I backed myself up against a massive tree. I continued hearing the footsteps until they suddenly stopped. I was somewhat panting, waiting for something to happen. Then I heard the oh so familiar breathing noise of a creature coming from behind the tree I was at.

I slowly went around it to be met with a bunch of flashlights in my face. "There you are, Mrs. Graives," Sergeant Major O'Hare stated in a worried but angry voice. "I thought I told you to stay close."

Oh, thank God! "Yeah, sorry. I somehow got turned

around."

"Well, we haven't found anything out here, so we're heading back. Let's go."

Within about a half hour we were back at the cabin. Some soldiers went to their tents to rest while others went back to their shifts. They set up camp outside the cabin, so it was rather convenient–and easy–during shift changes to go right to their respective tents.

Sergeant Ramirez escorted me back into the cabin. "Thank you, Sergeant."

"My pleasure, Ashlynn. Thank you for the amazing dinner."

I smiled. "Anytime, Sergeant."

He turned to go back to his tent while I went into the cabin. Jack was sitting on the couch as I walked in. "Anything?"

I shook my head. "No. I did accidently get separated from the team …"

He sat up. "Woah, what do you mean 'accidently' got separated?!"

I grimaced. "At one point, while we were searching, I looked up and noticed everyone was gone. That's when I heard footsteps and someone calling my name."

He shot up from the couch and came over to me. "Holy shit, are you okay?"

"Yes, I'm fine. We didn't find anything."

He relaxed. "Okay, good." But he was still standoffish.

"What's wrong?" I asked him.

"Nothing. I'm just tired. Let's go to bed," he responded in a rather unenthused voice and walked away.

Um, what the fuck?

I followed him. He went in, took off his shoes, and laid in bed as I walked in and closed the door. "No, seriously, what's going on, babe?"

"I don't know, you tell me."

I looked at him. "I'm sorry?"

"You talking to that soldier earlier."

I gave him a sly look. "Jealous?" He wasn't amused. "Oh, babe, seriously?! We were just talking. I was being hospitable since he was kind enough to fix the living room wall."

He calmed down a little. "I know and I'm sorry. Just seemed like you two were having a little *too* much fun."

I crossed my arms. "I want you to answer these two questions for me." He looked at me. "Who am I going to bed with tonight? Who am I madly in love with and married to?"

He sulked, knowing he was wrong. "Me," he mumbled.

"I'm sorry, what was that?" I asked, putting my hand to my ear, acting like I didn't hear him.

He repeated a little louder, "Me!"

"That's right!"

He smirked. "Come here," he said as he crooked his finger.

I beamed and sauntered over to him in a sexy manner. I stood next to him, brought my face close to his, and said, "Can I help you?"

"Yes, you can." He kissed me passionately.

I climbed on top of him, and we continued kissing. He moved his lips down my neck to my chest. As I enjoyed every touch, I happened to look over and noticed the curtains on the one window by us were still open and the blinds were up. I checked the other one behind me and it was open, as well. I sighed because I didn't want him to stop, but I said, "Uh, babe." He looked up at me. "The windows?"

He glanced at both. "What? You don't want the soldiers looking in and taking notes."

"More like I don't want them looking in and seeing me naked."

"Good point." He jumped out of bed and made sure the blinds were down and the curtains were closed on both windows before getting back in bed with me and continuing his journey.

JUNE 19th

This morning, I woke up and walked out to soldiers in my living room, kitchen, and pacing around outside. My tired eyes widened, and my sleepy brain immediately became alert. *What the ...?*

And then I remembered. *Oh, Jesus!*

I immediately wrapped my arms in front of me to cover myself up. I wasn't in a tank top and shorts; I was in a t-shirt and capri pants, but still. *I'm never going to get used to this! Hopefully, this doesn't last long!*

Sergeant Ramirez was standing in the kitchen, talking to another soldier. He looked over and saw me. "Good morning, Ashlynn," sounding all bright-eyed and bushy tailed.

Walking over to him, I grumbled, "Morning."

"You really aren't a morning person."

"Nope!" As I reached him, the other soldier walked away. I leaned closer to him and whispered, "And it doesn't help walking out to complete strangers in my home."

He laughed. "Well, hopefully this won't last long."

"I was just thinking that!"

We both laughed. I offered him coffee and breakfast, but he politely refused. "I already had my breakfast bar but thank you."

I nodded. "Sounds good. I think I'm going to change first, though, before I go around asking everyone else if they want anything."

Sergeant Ramirez chuckled. "Not a bad idea."

I powerwalked back to my room. Jack was just waking up and saw me. He groaned, "Again?"

"What? I'm not used to this."

"Um … what about the crew?"

"Oh, please, I'm dressed way before any of them are up."

He was about to say something but stopped. "True."

About a half hour later, I went back out—with Jack by my side—and checked with every soldier if I could offer them something, anything. They all refused, but some weren't as kind as others. *All right, I'm going to start making a mental note of those of you who have been rude to me the past couple of days and walk right by you instead of checking in!*

Little by little, the crew began coming out of their little caves. We went about our day as if there wasn't a legit army surrounding us for the third (or fourth? I lost count) day in a row. We haven't seen anything or heard anything in those days. Nothing from Cillian; nothing from his goons. My boys visited the other day, saying they were on the hunt for Cillian, but found nothing.

Today, I was so freaking bored, I decided to go for a swim. With everything going on, I just needed some time to myself, and being in the lake was always my little sanctuary away from the craziness. I put on a swimsuit, grabbed a towel, and headed out. As I was walking toward the lake, one of the soldiers stopped me. "And where do you think you're going?"

I looked at him. "Into the lake for a swim. Problem?"

"Yeah, we need to be watching over you to make sure no harm comes to you."

"Well, I don't think anything is going to happen to me in the middle of this lake." I began walking away.

He shouted, "How do you know?"

I turned toward him, ready to fight. "Look …"

Then from behind me I heard, "We'll watch over her."

I whipped around and saw my boys. I was so elated to see them. I ran over and gave each of them a hug. "Thank God you guys are here. I was ready to punch him out."

Kaden replied, "And be put in jail for the rest of your life."

"Yeah, but it would be *so* worth it!"

We all laughed. Roman said, "So, I see you're about to go for a swim." He eyed me up and down, gawking at me like I was a piece of meat.

Kaden and Glen sighed and shook their heads. I slapped him on his arm. "Hey!" He looked at me. "Up here," I said, pointing at my eyes.

"What? You look terrific!"

"Thanks, but still. Taken, bitch," I responded, showing off my left ring finger. No, I don't wear my rings in the lake, but I have a rubber one I wear pretty much all the time, except for special occasions.

He muttered, "Thanks for the reminder."

I laughed. "But, yes, I am going for a swim. I need to. This," gesturing toward the cabin and the soldiers, "is slowly killing me. I need to breathe and relax."

Kaden came over and wrapped his arm around my shoulders as we walked toward the lake. "Don't worry, sweetie. Like I said, we'll watch over you. We can't really swim anyway."

I gaped up at him. "So how the hell are you going to help me if I get attacked?"

"No, I mean 'we' as in 'we monsters.'"

I smacked him. "What did I say about calling yourselves

monsters?"

He rolled his eyes. "You know what I mean."

I shook my head. "Well, I was going in no matter what, so hopefully the others can't swim. But I won't go out too far."

"Good idea," they said in unison.

Before heading in, I asked, "Did you guys find anything?"

They shook their heads. I sighed. "I was afraid of that."

Kaden rubbed my back. "Don't worry, hon. We're taking a break now, but we'll get back to it in a little bit."

I gave a half smile and nodded. I dropped my towel, took off my sandals, and started walking in only to be stalled. "Holy shit, that's cold!" I shouted.

The boys laughed. That's when Jack came out. "Babe, it may be the middle of June, but that doesn't mean the water is going to be warm. What, did you think it was going to be the same temperature as the air?"

"Fuck you, babe." I flipped him off.

"Love you, too."

Glen came over to me. "Here, let me help you out, sis!" He picked me up and started walking into the lake.

I screamed. "No, Glen! Put me down! Jack!"

"I'm sorry, babe! He's much bigger than me now!"

Glen walked into the lake a little more, to where the water was just above his waist, and asked, "Do you want me to put you down?"

"Yes!" I hollered.

"Okay." He then tossed me in. Wanna talk about a shock to your fucking system?! Damn, that water was cold!

I surfaced to find everyone, including a couple of the soldiers, laughing their asses off. "I hate you all *sooo* much!"

Once he was able to breathe again from laughing so hard, Glen said, "Love you, Ash!"

I tittered. "Yeah, yeah, love you, too, ass!"

I swam away as he went back to Jack, Roman, and Kaden. I continued swimming for a little while longer before just lying in the water and taking in its calmness—not hearing anything except for my breathing, a light breeze blowing, and some birds chirping. It was so peaceful. It reminded me of why I loved that area. After God knows how long, I heard, "Um … I thought you were going to stay close!"

I sat up, treading in the water, to notice I was a good twenty or thirty yards away from the shore. *Ah, crap!* "Well, how am I supposed to pay attention to where I'm going when I'm just drifting?"

That's when Sergeant Major O'Hare came stomping toward the lake. "You can't be out that far, Mrs. Graives! You need to come back here, now!" he barked.

I mimicked him as I started paddling back.

"Now, Mrs. Graives," he ordered.

"Okay, I'm heading back!" I shouted. "Damn."

Just as I was about to really start swimming, I heard a branch crack. I stopped and looked over to my right. I was pretty close to shore on that side, but ahead of me, I was still pretty far out. I thought I saw something moving. I continued staring.

"Mrs. Graives, don't make me tell you again!"

Then a pair of lids opened, and I saw two fire red eyes staring at me. I gasped. *Oh, shit!*

The creature and I stared at each other for some time before it decided to take a step toward me, and then another … and another. Other than my feet kicking to keep me afloat, I was frozen in fear. I didn't know who this was. It obviously wasn't Cillian, but who could it be? I was praying it wasn't Nash.

I heard the guys and soldiers screaming my name, urging me to swim back slowly, but I just … couldn't … move. Then my boys started roaring, "Stay away from her!"

That's when I realized the creature wasn't reacting to their calls. Either it was completely ignoring them, or … "Mikey?" The creature stopped mid-stride, only a few feet away from me. "Mikey, is that you?"

He waved at me. My heart sank. *Oh, Jesus! Not you, too!*

Mikey was a bartender at The Lake's Drinking Hole, the bar in Nonoma, who's deaf, but he can read lips really well. I noticed he wasn't working when the boys and I went–before all this bullshit started–and I asked about him. According to one of the other bartenders, he thought he just up and left. "I guess he moved on to bigger and better things," he said. Well, now I know what happened to him. Only God knows why Mr. MacReedy took him to the lab "to be worked on." I felt horrible.

I said to him, "Mikey, we have missed you, bud. We wondered where you were."

He signed, "Sheriff MacReedy took me away. Told me he would help me, but he did not. I was tortured and changed into this." He gestured to himself.

I learned how to read and sign for Mikey. He was always so kind to Glen, my parents, and myself. It was the least I could do to talk to him "properly."

Everything became quiet as Glen realized who it was, from the signing, and told everyone to stop as their efforts would be fruitless. My heart raced. I started, "I …" as he continued walking toward me. He signed, "He said it is because of you."

He reached out, grabbed my left wrist, and pulled me toward him, holding me up a little bit by my right elbow. I heard Jack yell, "Ashlynn!"

Heavily breathing, I looked at him and said, "Mikey, I did not know. I am sorry."

He let go of my wrist to sign, "He wants you."

I vigorously shook my head. "No, Mikey, please …"

He then picked me up and put me over his shoulder. I screamed, "No! Jack!"

I fought, pushing and punching Mikey in the back, but I barely budged off his shoulder. I looked up to see Jack fighting to get to me, but the boys were holding him back. I also saw the soldiers lined up with their guns at the ready, but Sergeant Major ordered, "Don't shoot!"

I continued punching and kicking as Mikey was heading into deeper waters. "I thought you guys couldn't swim," I said, baffled at what was happening.

Then, at one point, I elbowed him (with my bad elbow, of course) in the back of the head, and it must've hurt because he dropped me and held his head. After coming up, I winced in pain and held my elbow for a hot second before I started swimming as fast as I could. I looked up to see Jack and my boys, encouraging me to swim faster, harder. I looked back to see Mikey turning toward me. I became Dory and screamed in my head, "Just keep swimming! Just keep swimming!"

But I didn't get far before I felt a hand wrap around my ankle and pull me back. Mikey grabbed me by the back of my neck and held me up. For a second, I thought he was going to dunk my head in the lake and try to drown me, but I remembered he's not that type of person. I pleaded, making sure he saw my mouth, "Mikey, please let me go. He is a bad man. He will hurt me."

He signed, "No, he is good. He saved me. He has protected me."

"Protected you from what? Them?" I pointed to the soldiers lining the shore. He looked up and growled. I waved so he could look back at me. "They are not the enemy, Mikey. He is. He is a very bad man."

I could see in Mikey's eyes he was conflicted. Only God knows what Cillian has been telling him. I decided to start signing because I knew Mikey appreciated it more when you signed to him. That way he didn't have to concentrate on your lips. He feared it spooked people because he would just be staring, meanwhile he was literally seeing what you were saying. I signed, "They will not harm you. I will make sure of it."

"Promise?"

"I promise. But you have to let me go."

He slowly loosened his grip on my neck and put me down. Once I was free, I waved to everyone on shore and yelled, "Don't shoot! He's not going to harm me, and he won't harm you!"

I heard Sergeant Major instruct, "Stand down," and saw the soldiers relax their arms.

Jack hollered, "Are you okay?"

"Yes, I'm fine," I answered as I rubbed my neck.

I turned toward Mikey and signed, "Come with me. Everything will be okay."

"But he will be upset. I did not do what I was told. He will hurt me."

I became upset and exclaimed, "No, he won't! I won't let

him!"

He once again signed, "Promise?"

I said and signed, "Promise." I smiled and he smiled back. "Come on."

I started swimming as he walked. Then I heard something from behind us. It was like a small splash. I turned and looked around. Mikey turned with me. I looked at him and he signed, "Did you hear something?"

I nodded. We looked around. Suddenly, this force came up, out of the water. It was Cillian. He grabbed Mikey and shoved him down. "NO!" I screamed. "Mikey!"

I dove under to try and save him, even though I knew there was nothing I could really do. I barely saw anything, the water was so murky, but I could tell there was a struggle going on. I went back up for air. "Mikey!"

I panned over to see everyone telling me to get back to shore. I didn't want to leave him, but at the same time I knew I couldn't save him, no matter how hard I tried. I once again started swimming back only to notice that when I kicked up the water, it was dark red. I stopped and looked around myself. I was surrounded by blood. Whose? I could only guess Mikey's. I screamed again. Then I felt a hand wrap around my calf. I looked up and screamed, "Jack!" as I was pulled under water. I felt massive hands wrap around my neck and looked up to see Cillian. He was holding me down. I fought, forgetting that by doing so, I would black out more quickly ... and I did.

****

I awoke in the middle of the woods; it was dark out. I looked around to see if I could figure out where I was, but I didn't recognize anything. That's when I threw up the water I had swallowed from Cillian holding me down. I was so disoriented. I took a moment to breathe and settle myself. I was dry, but I was freezing. The temperature dropped considerably, and I couldn't stop shivering. I looked around, trying to figure out where I was. The lake wasn't anywhere in sight. I saw no cabins, no lights, nothing! There may have been a full moon, but all I saw were trees and beyond a certain point, darkness.

I slowly got up off the ground. I continued looking around to see where Cillian was. I still saw nothing. There wasn't even a sound. No insects, no bats, just ... pure ... silence.

I quivered, not only from the cold but from fear. I wrapped my arms around myself to try and stay warm. Then I started hearing my name being called from what seemed to be a far distance. I was about to yell back when a figure stepped out from behind a tree, those damn red eyes staring at me. I knew it wasn't one of my boys, but thankfully, it also wasn't Cillian. I had no clue who it was until he smirked and said, "Well, hello, beautiful."

"Nash?"

"That's right, sexy."

I immediately wasn't as afraid anymore. "I was hoping my boys left you for dead."

His smile disappeared. "This," he pointed to his face, "is all because of you."

"Fuck you! I didn't know! I didn't know the sheriff was taking people and experimenting on them!"

"Bullshit!" He started walking toward me.

I backed away, knowing what he could possibly do to me, but I ran into a tree. I continued to stand my ground, though.

"Really, asshole?! Think about it for a second! My brothers were experimented on, as well!"

As he reached me, he said, "Yeah, you sent them to that lab so you could get some love and affection, you attention-seeking whore!"

"You son of a ..."

I took a swing at him, but he grabbed my wrist and held it tight. I winced in pain. "What the hell are you going to do? Knock me out? You don't have a big branch to protect you this time." I struggled, and as I did, I saw blood trickling down my arm. It truly reminded me of that night a little over a year and half ago. "No, my dear," he caressed my cheek, "let me show you how to punch." He wound up, but before he could follow through, something stopped him. We both looked up to see Cillian, who was mad as hell. Nash immediately let go of my wrist. I held it to my chest as I continued cringing in pain, my forearm covered in blood. "Cillian ... I ...," Nash stuttered.

Cillian bellowed, "You have pissed me off for the last time, Nash!"

He picked him up like he was a rag doll, lifted him over his head, and literally ripped him apart. His blood sprayed everywhere including all over me. I screamed. Cillian threw Nash's two halves down and covered my mouth with his blood-soaked hand. "Sh ... don't make another sound or ..." he took his hand away from my mouth and wrapped it around my neck. Not so tight that I couldn't breathe, but tight enough to make his point. He said, "I'll snap your neck like a twig. Got it?"

I nodded as my eyes and face grew hot from tears welling up. I was once again frightened, but I did all I could to make sure those tears didn't roll down my cheeks. He took his hand off my neck and caressed my cheek. "My love."

My heart skipped a beat. Trying my hardest to sound strong, I asked, "What do you want, Cillian?"

"Isn't it obvious?" He leaned in closer and whispered into my ear, "You."

I couldn't help it. The tears started rolling. My voice cracked, "Why me?"

He explained, "Every time I heard Kaden, Roman, and Glen talk about you, I just had to find you to see what all the hype was about. And then when we escaped that wretched lab and I found you," he pushed the hair off my shoulder. "Well, I guess you can say it was love at first sight." I almost retched. "I just had to have you; I had to be with you. But when I saw you left, I came up with a plan to get you back here and what better way than by attacking a place you love so much. And now, I can finally touch you." He glided a finger up and down my arm. "I can finally have you. I can finally …" He placed a hand around my waist and pulled me into him. With his free hand, he placed his index finger on my chin to force me to look up at him. "… kiss you," and he did. The son of a bitch kissed me.

I wanted to fight back, but I knew he was too strong for me. I just stayed in place, breathing heavily, tears cascading down my cheeks. I couldn't believe this was happening. It's one of those things you never imagine happening to you, especially with a freaking monster, but there I was, face to face with my worst fear. I was so numb with terror that I didn't do anything. I barely reciprocated the kiss. He looked at me and saw the tears. "Aw, baby." He tenderly wiped them from my cheeks. "Don't worry, I'll be gentle."

I put on the bravest face I could and glared at him as he continued caressing my face. "That's sweet, but I'm taken."

"Ha! One night with me and you'll leave that human."

"That human?" Jesus, he really does think he's a god!

"No, thanks."

He glowered at me. He pushed me, hard, into the tree and once again, grabbed my neck, this time with a little more pressure. "I have no problem forcing you to see, my love!"

That's when, from behind him, we heard, "Let the girl go, Cillian!"

He let go of me. I coughed as I caught my breath. He turned around–and I looked around him–to see Sergeant Major O'Hare and his troops, their guns up. Then behind them I saw my man. "Jack!" I came around and tried running to him, but Cillian grabbed me by my arm and pulled me back.

"Ashlynn!" He tried running to me, but one of my boys held him back saying, "Hold on, bud, hold on." I think it was Roman.

Jack yelled, "Let her go, asshole!"

Cillian growled. Sergeant Major continued, "She said, 'No!' Now let her go, Cillian!"

"Or what the hell are you going to do, O'Hare? Shoot me? You know your puny bullets will do nothing to me."

He pushed me aside and started walking toward them.

Sergeant Major yelled, "Ashlynn, duck!" I immediately ran behind a tree. "FIRE!"

Gunfire filled the forest. It was like being under fireworks during the Fourth of July, it was so deafening. I covered my ears and peeked around the tree trunk to see what was going on. I couldn't believe it; this guy was truly the fucking Hulk! The bullets seemed to bounce off him, but it didn't take long before his skin began to weaken and some bullets were starting to wound him, his blood splattering everywhere. Eventually, he ran off in pain. Most of the soldiers followed him, but I don't think it was long before they lost him. His stride was the equivalent of 5'6" me taking like ten steps.

I came around the tree to Jack. I wrapped my arms around his neck. He picked me up and held me. "Oh, thank God! Are you okay, baby?"

I cried, "Yes! Oh, Jack!"

"Sh, it's okay! I got you now!"

We both cried as we held each other, forgetting I was covered in blood. That's when I felt something wrap around me. I looked over to see Sergeant Major giving me his coat. "Here, Mrs. Graives. Everything will be okay."

I let go of Jack, who helped me put the coat on. Seeing my face, he gasped. "Oh, Jesus, babe." He took the sleeve of his sweater and wiped my face.

"Thank you, baby." I looked over at Sergeant Major O'Hare. "Thank you, Sergeant Major."

He nodded. "My pleasure, Mrs. Graives. I'm just glad we reached you in the nick of time."

"Yeah, me, too."

We then heard someone clearing their throat behind us. We turned to see Roman standing a few feet away. "Hey, babe."

I ran over to him and jumped into his arms. He held me as I wept. "Thank you for not running after him."

"Oh, trust me, it took everything in me not to, but I knew you needed me here."

He held me for a little bit longer before putting me down. Jack came up from behind me, placed a hand on my shoulder, and said, "Come on, babe. Let's go back to the cabin and get you cleaned up."

We all started walking, Jack's arm around my shoulders. I asked, "Where are Glen and Kaden?"

Roman answered, "They stayed back at the cabin, waiting to see if you would show up there."

I smiled. "Like how I did for you guys."

"Yup."

"So, may I ask, why you? Why did you come out with Jack?"

He gasped and sarcastically replied, "Ashlynn Angela Graives, I'm hurt." We all laughed. "But I did it because I wanted to be there for Jack." I looked up at him, somewhat doubting him. "I know I've given him a lot of grief."

"You mean you've been a massive pain in the ass to him," I chimed in.

He paused. "Yes, I've been a massive asshole to him, but when I saw the pain in his eyes as he was forced to watch Cillian walk away with you, I realized how much he truly loves you. I found a new respect for him, and I wanted to be by his side when we found you." He patted Jack on the shoulder.

Jack smiled. "Thanks, man. I truly appreciate it."

"No problem."

My heart fluttered. "Roman, I think you've finally grown up."

"Uh, I wouldn't go that far."

We all laughed again as we continued our trek back home.

****

Just as we came over the hill, we heard, "There they are!"

I looked up to see Glen and Kaden running toward us. I let go of Jack and ran for them, jumping right into Glen's arms. I started bawling, happy to be back with my baby brother.

"Oh, thank God you're okay, Ash." I wrapped my arms tighter around him and just cried. But, of course, he had to joke, "Because I don't think I could explain this one to Mom and Dad. I would actually get in trouble, for once."

I laughed. "You ass!"

He put me down and I went over to Kaden. He hugged me tight. "Are you sure you're okay, hon?"

I nodded. He let go and looked at me. "Then who's blood is this?"

"Nash's."

They gawked at me. "What?" they said in unison.

"Nash was about to hit me when Cillian stopped him and ripped him in half. His blood splattered all over," I explained, becoming hysterical.

Kaden pulled me in tight and Glen caressed my head. "You're okay, now. You're safe with us and we're not going anywhere," Glen declared.

I continued crying into Kaden's chest when Jack said, "Come on, baby. Let's get you inside."

Just as I picked up my head and let go of Kaden, Glen said, "Actually, there's someone here who was helping us try to find you. You don't want him to see you like this."

I looked at Glen, confused. "Who's here?"

"Mr. Scarlo."

My heart melted. "Aw." And then I remembered, "Oh, shit, yeah, he can't see me like this!"

Jack came around and asked, "Do you want me to run down and explain the situation?"

"Please, babe. I would really appreciate that."

"You got it," and he started running toward the cabin.

Then it hit me. "Wait ... Mr. Scarlo saw you like this," pointing to his new form. Glen nodded. "And he didn't freak out?"

"Oh, he freaked out. Not as bad as I was expecting because you know how he can be."

I nodded feverishly. "Yeah, I do!"

"But yeah, he saw what happened and he wanted to do whatever he could to help."

"Aw, he truly is a good guy."

"Wait, wait, wait ... who the hell is Mr. Scarlo?" Roman asked from behind us.

I turned to face him. "He's a family-friend who's a little on the ... flamboyant side."

"How bad is he?"

I answered, "He makes Kaden look straight."

They all howled with laughter. Roman said, in between trying to catch his breath, "I can't wait to meet this guy."

We resumed our walk back to the cabin. Glen was to my right, Roman to my left, and Kaden was behind me making sure nothing happened to me, making sure Cillian didn't try to get me again.

As we got closer, I could hear Mr. Scarlo screaming, "I don't care if she's covered in shit!"

I halted so fast, Kaden bumped into me. "Oh, honey, I'm sorry. What's the matter?"

They all looked at me. My eyes were practically popping out of my head, and my mouth was almost touching the forest floor. Kaden asked, "Ash, you okay?"

I finally answered, "Yeah, I've just never heard Mr. Scarlo curse before. He's always yelled at me for cursing."

Kaden rubbed my shoulders. "He was really concerned about you, hon."

I waited a moment before continuing. Mr. Scarlo must've seen me coming from behind Jack because I heard, "Ashlynn," and then saw him practically flying toward me with his arms reaching out. I never saw him run so quickly. As he reached me, he wrapped his arms around me, tight. "Oh, sweetie, I'm so happy to see you safe! Are you okay?"

I matched his hug, ecstatic to see him since it had been a while. "I'm fine, Mr. Scarlo. Thank you so much for being here."

"Of course, sweetie. You're like a daughter to me."

We held each other for another few seconds. He let go and I asked him, "Not to sound horribly mean, Mr. Scarlo, because I'm truly appreciative that you're here, but what are you doing back in Lake Minnetaha? I thought you were never coming back."

"Well, that was the plan, but David brought up a good point that we need to fix up the cabin a little before selling it. You know, make it look presentable."

I agreed, "Makes sense."

"So …"

Before Mr. Scarlo could continue with his story, Sergeant Major O'Hare came up to us and said, "Please forgive me, Ms. Ashlynn, but I would prefer if everyone was inside to keep you all safe."

I was kind of astonished he called me Ms. Ashlynn instead of Mrs. Graives, but he was right. "No, you're fine, Sergeant Major. Thank you. Oh, and …"

I started to take off his jacket, but he stopped me. "No, keep it for now until you're all cleaned up and settled."

I nodded. "Thank you again, sir."

We went into the cabin. Chad, Greg, Jerry, and even Sergeant Ramirez greeted me with a hug and checked in. Jerry asked, "Anything I should be concerned about?"

Then I recalled. "Yeah, my right wrist. It's not bothering me right now, but it was bleeding earlier."

They all yelled, "Bleeding?!"

I jumped a little. "Once again with the echoes."

Jack asked, "From what?"

When I told them what happened, my boys fumed. "It's a good thing Cillian ripped that fucker in half, or I would've," Roman responded through gritted teeth.

Mr. Scarlo spoke up. "I'm sorry, I haven't met you yet, but please no cursing, especially in front of my Ashlynn."

Roman cocked his head to one side. "I'm sorry?"

Oh, crap!

I put my hand up and explained, "Mr. Scarlo is not a big fan of profanity." Then I looked at him. "Even though I just heard you say a curse word."

Mr. Scarlo became as red as a tomato; he was so embarrassed. "Oh, sugar, you heard me?"

"Yup!" I answered with a big, shit-eating grin on my face.

He implored me for forgiveness. "I'm so sorry, sweetie. I was just so concerned about you."

I laughed. "It's okay, Mr. Scarlo. But I do need to ask … how do you feel after cursing? Are you okay? Do you need to lie down?"

We all started laughing and I started feeling better, not totally but somewhat forgetting the ordeal I was just in. Once we all composed ourselves, Jerry said, "When you're ready to get cleaned up, I'll take a look at your arm and see what we're dealing with."

"Sounds good, Doc."

Mr. Scarlo said, "Well, why don't you go and get cleaned up, sweetie, and I'll make all of us some tea, that way you're not staying like that."

He walked away and went toward the kitchen. I followed him, feeling a little worried. "Uh, which tea are you going to make, Mr. Scarlo?"

As he reached the kitchen, grabbed the tea pot, and started putting water in it, he answered, "You and I are getting my tea because we *so* need it right now and everyone else can have whatever they want."

Kaden asked, "What's in your tea, Mr. Scarlo?"

Both Mr. Scarlo and I turned to him and said, "Don't ask."

I looked back at Mr. Scarlo and politely said, "Thank you for the offer, M…"

"Oh, it's not an offer, sweetie," he interrupted me, turning off the water and putting the pot on the stove. "You're having some. Trust me, you need it."

"But … I want to wake up tomorrow, Mr. Scarlo."

He laughed. "And you will. I won't make it as potent as I usually do." I stared at him blankly, wondering how the hell he's going to make his tea less potent than normal. He placed his hand on my shoulder and said, "Don't worry, sweetie. You'll be fine. Now go get cleaned up."

I smiled, turned, and walked away, somewhat relieved, but also knowing that I'm probably not going to see the light of day until next week.

JUNE 20th

Well, I was somewhat right. I didn't wake up until around noon. All I remember from last night is going into the bathroom, Jack and Jerry looking at my arm–which had some cuts and bruising, but nothing worse, thankfully–and Mr. Scarlo and I sitting on the couch, catching up as we drank his tea. He told me how him and his husband, David literally got into town yesterday and started opening up the windows in their cabin to let in some fresh air when they heard a scream. They looked out their bedroom window, which faces the lake, and saw me being carried away by some gigantic creature while hearing Jack screaming my name. "Well, I immediately got into the car, while David stayed at the cabin, and rushed over to only be greeted by soldiers with guns."

I apologized for the "lovely" greeting and realized we probably should've added, "We will not point our guns at any civilians that may visit the cabin while we are stationed here," to the contract.

I told him, "You know, I'm a little disappointed David didn't come with you. I still need to meet your man."

"I know, but he decided it would be best, just in case anyone or anything came to the cabin. He could protect it."

"Fair enough."

Mr. Scarlo continued, "Anyway, thankfully, Glen came over and told them to put their guns down, but I didn't recognize him, obviously. It took me some time to … adjust I guess you can say."

I remember agreeing with him and him saying he joined in the search and that was about it. By that point, I was starting to feel good and so was Mr. Scarlo. We said our goodbyes and Sergeant Major had a few of his soldiers escort him back to his cabin and stand watch, just to be safe.

I have to admit, when I first met Sergeant Major O'Hare, I thought he was a tyrannical asshole, but now … I'm seeing him in a totally different light. He, of course, puts up this front, but he's a good man. He, Sergeant Ramirez, and most of his platoon are actually all good guys. *So, how the hell did they get wrapped up in all this shit?*

Once I was fully awake, I called Mr. Scarlo to make sure he was okay. He said they were fine, but they were leaving. David convinced him it's not safe to stay right now with everything going on. He suggested I do the same. "I'll think about," I responded.

"I know you all too well, Ashlynn, and that means you're staying. Why, I'll never understand, but please be safe, sweetie."

"I will. Thank you, Mr. Scarlo. And please offer my apologies to David. I …"

Before I said anything else, I heard David exclaim, "No need to apologize, Ash! I'm just glad you're safe."

"Thank you, David. Hopefully, one day I can meet you."

"I can't wait to do so, honey."

After my conversation with Mr. Scarlo, Jack and I went and sat on the couch in the living room. I rested my legs on top of his and he wrapped his arm around my shoulders as we watched TV. Things were going pretty well until we heard a commotion outside. "You're not allowed to be here! Who the hell do you think you are?"

"You know exactly who the hell I am, Sergeant Major!"

I looked at Jack. "Oh, hell no!" I was hoping to never hear that Texas accent ever again.

Jack and I shot up and ran outside. Sergeant Major, his back to us, turned and said, "I'm sorry, Ms. Ashlynn, I'm trying to get him to leave the premises, but ..."

That son of a bitch looked around the sergeant major, smiled at me, and said, "Oh, Ms. Ashlynn, I'm so happy to see you, darlin'. How have you been?"

Jack started, "You have no right ..." but I stopped him and looked at him, trying to tell him in our own special way that I got this. He understood and backed down.

"What the hell do you want, Mr. MacReedy?" I asked in a harsh, monotone voice. I wanted to make sure he understood he wasn't welcome.

His smile immediately disappeared. "Well, I was hoping we could maybe talk and catch up, like the good ol' days."

I raged inside. I was about to answer when my boys came around from the back of the cabin. Kaden asked, "What's going ..." and then they saw him. Roman started to rush at him, but Kaden, Glen, Jack, and some soldiers did all they could to hold him back. I even stepped in front of him and said, "Back off, Roman! I got this!"

"This motherfucker took our lives away!"

I walked over to him and said, "No, seriously, I got this. Stand down." He looked at me. "Please."

He huffed and relaxed his stance, enough for everyone to let him go. He pointed at Mr. MacReedy. "You're lucky she's here, asshole, or you would be a dead man right now."

I barked, "Roman stop!"

"Fine!"

I went back over to Mr. MacReedy. "So let me get this straight; I want to make sure I heard you correctly. You said you want us to sit down and catch up 'like the good ol' days'?"

He nodded and practically whimpered, "Please, darlin'. I have nowhere else to go. I have no one to turn to."

"Not my fucking problem that your lucrative side business went sour. Maybe you shouldn't have done deals with the government and sold people's lives for cash."

"I thought I was doing the right thing. I thought I was getting punks off the street."

"And have them turned into super soldiers?! How the hell is that any better?!"

"Because they would then be disciplined by these fine soldiers," he replied, pointing to the servicemen surrounding my boys.

Sergeant Major became irate. "Oh, now you want to kiss ass?"

"I'm not kissing ass; I'm just speaking the truth."

I took a couple of deep breaths in, doing all I could to not pounce on this dirt bag and start beating the living shit out of him. "Mr. MacReedy, if I were you, I would turn around, leave here, and never return. You are not welcome here any longer."

I went to walk away when he cried, "Please, Ms. Ashlynn, don't leave this old man to rot. There was a point in time you said you would've been with me if you didn't have your eyes on Jack."

I turned back around and rushed at him, foaming at the mouth with anger. Jack grabbed me around my waist to hold me back. "Babe ..."

I screamed, "Don't you ever say my husband's name again!"

Mr. MacReedy took a step back—even Sergeant Major flinched a little, shocked at my fury. "Okay, Ms. Ashlynn, I'm sorry. But you did say that."

I lowered my voice and replied, "I also once said that Meredith was the luckiest woman in the world to have had you as a husband, but clearly I was wrong." I knew my remark hit hard when I saw his lower lip quiver and a few tears roll down his cheeks. Now, don't think of me as a complete monster because I did feel horrible for saying it, but at the same time I was just as hurt and angry for what he did to us; for taking my boys away and turning them into the creatures they are now.

I felt tears welling up in my eyes and a lump coming up my throat, but I choked it back and said, "Now, get off my property and never come back."

I turned and went toward the cabin. Mr. MacReedy yelled out, "Please, Ms. Ashlynn. He's going to kill me. Please help me."

I stopped for a moment, but then continued into the cabin, followed by Jack, and literally everyone else, except for any soldiers who were stationed outside. They went back to their posts.

Before going toward our room, I stopped, looked at Jack, and said, "I need a moment."

"Okay, baby," he responded, and just let me be.

I went into our room and silently wailed. I didn't want anyone to know I was shedding tears for that bastard. Not tears of sadness, but tears of pure rage and pain. I hoped, I prayed I would never see him again. And for him to come back and beg for my help was … just … outrageous! But when he said, "He's going to kill me," my heart sank down into my stomach. My fear skyrocketed. I knew what he meant; we all knew what he meant. But I just couldn't easily forgive him for what he did.

With my head buried in my hands, I heard the door open. I pleaded, "Please, Jack, I just want …" I panned up and saw my boys. I didn't say one word to them, and they didn't say a word to me. They just came over and sat with me. I wrapped my arms around Kaden, Glen rested his head on my shoulder, and Roman gently rubbed my back as I continued to cry.

JUNE 23rd

I was asleep when I was startled awake by a weird noise. As I slowly rose, the noise became clearer; it was the same scratching noise I had heard when I was introduced to the monsters. However, this time it was different. This time I was able to follow the noise from above my head as it came around the room. I fully sat up in bed as I followed it.

Suddenly, it stopped in the exact same spot where we originally found the marks a year and a half ago–and so did my breathing. I sat there, my heart racing, wondering what was going to happen next. That's when a huge, charred fist broke through the wall. I jumped and screamed. I began shaking Jack violently, shouting, "He's here! Jack, he's here!" But he didn't move.

Then Cillian burst through like the wall wasn't even there. I turned and stared, frozen in place. He looked at me with those devil-red eyes of his and smiled from ear to ear. "My love," he said.

As I stared at him, I noticed he was dragging something behind him. It looked like a person. He looked down at it, looked back up at me, and said, "A present for you."

He tossed the body onto the bed. I looked down to see the lifeless eyes of Mr. MacReedy staring up at me, his face smeared with blood. I screamed. Cillian walked over to me. I watched him as he got closer and closer. I still didn't move, other than my head cranking up to look at him. I was like a deer in fucking headlights, my breathing labored. As he reached me, he caressed my cheek and said, "You're finally mine!"

I screamed again as everything went black.

****

I woke up, dripping in sweat and yelling from the top of my lungs as Jack shook me, exclaiming, "Ashlynn, it's only a dream!"

I shot up in our bed, taking in air like I had just run a marathon. I looked around. It was morning. Thankfully, Cillian was nowhere in sight, or at least as far as I knew. Jack caressed my head and repeated, "It's okay, it's okay."

I fell into him and balled, "Oh, Jack. I'm so scared."

He held me and said, "It's okay, baby. I got you."

It had been a few days since Cillian kidnapped me. The first night after it happened, I didn't have any dreams, thanks to Mr. Scarlo's tea. But ever since then, I've been having nightmares that have been getting worse and worse and they all involve Cillian getting to me. However, this was the first night Mr. MacReedy showed up, dead.

I'm sure you're wondering why the hell I stayed and didn't go home. Well, it's because I know the destruction, the chaos, none of it will stop until Cillian is found and captured. I guess you can say it's become my mission to find him—and any other creatures—and stop them. However, I am absolutely *filled* with fear.

Once I calmed down, Jack asked, "What can I get you, babe? Do you want anything to eat or drink?"

"I guess some tea would be nice."

"Sure. Anything in particular?"

"Well, I wish Mr. Scarlo left some of his tea, so I wouldn't have these damn nightmares." He chortled as he rubbed my back. "But some chamomile would be helpful."

He smiled and said, "You got it." He gave me a kiss and headed out our bedroom door toward the kitchen.

I went back to staring at the wall where Cillian came through in my dream. For the first time ever in my life, I didn't want to be in that cabin; I didn't want to be in a place I considered my second home. All I wanted to do was go home. But, like I said, I had a mission.

As I continued sitting on our bed, I pushed my knees to my chest, wrapped my arms around my legs, buried my head, and cried. After some time, I heard heavy footsteps coming toward the room. I looked up to see my boys coming in. "Hey, hon," Kaden said.

"Hey," I replied in a low, almost whisper-like voice.

"Another bad dream, sis?" Glen asked.

I nodded and cried some more.

They all came over and sat with me. "Same one you've been having?" Roman questioned.

"Yeah, but this time Cillian gave me Mr. MacReedy's dead body as a gift." They all gasped. "His face was all bloody and his eyes … oh, god, his eyes."

Kaden pulled me into him. Glen rubbed my back while Roman just had to open his goddamn mouth. "Good. Maybe that means the fucker got what he deserved."

We all bellowed, "ROMAN!"

"What?! You all know me by now! Why are you constantly shocked by what I say?"

Glen retorted, "Yeah, but dude, we're talking about a person's life possibly being taken."

"Yeah, a person who caused us to become *this*," he

gestured to himself, his transformed body.

We all shook our heads in disgust.

Moments later, Jack came in. "Do you want the tea in here, babe, or out in the dining room?"

"Dining room, please. I'll get out of bed in a minute."

"You got it, babe."

He walked away as I forced myself off Kaden. He stood up so I could get up. He said, "You know, hon, no one would blame you if you just stayed in bed."

I shrugged. "As opposed to me lying on the couch all day?"

"At least your bed is comfy."

I snorted a little. "I needed that. Thank you."

"Of course, hon," he replied while rubbing my back.

I grabbed my robe, put it on, and went out into the kitchen. I met Jack as he handed me my tea. I looked around and saw some of the soldiers staring at me with empathy in their eyes while others either looked down, looked outside, or just looked somewhere else completely. I don't know if it was their way of saying, "Yeah, don't care what you're going through," or, "I know you must be embarrassed, so I'm not going to stare at you," but either way, I kind of appreciated it. Sergeant Ramirez came up to me and asked, "How are you doing, Ashlynn?"

"I mean, other than having another lovely nightmare, I guess I'm doing okay."

He smiled a little. "Glad to hear ... that you're doing okay, not that you had another ..."

I kindly interrupted him, "It's totally fine, Sergeant. I understood what you meant."

He nodded. "Plan on staying in again?"

Ever since everything happened, I've become a hermit. As much as I want to go for a walk in the backyard, or go for a swim in the lake, or even help the soldiers search for Cillian and the others, I'm too frightened to do so. I'm fearful that Cillian would get me again. Yes, I have my boys who would protect me, but I wasn't about to put them in danger.

"I guess," I answered, gazing at my tea.

"If you don't mind me saying, Ash, you do need to get out. You need to face your fear. A gentleman by the name of W. Clement Stone once said, 'Thinking will not overcome fear, but action will.'" I looked up at him. "Sitting around is not going to solve your problem and it's definitely not going to get rid of the fear you have. But by taking action, by taking steps to face that fear, you will come out stronger than Cillian could ever be."

I smiled. "You know, you remind me so much of Kaden." I turned and looked at him. He winked at me.

Ramirez asked, "How so, ma'am?"

As I continued looking at him, I said, "He always gives such amazing advice." Even though you couldn't really see it, I knew he was blushing. I looked back over at Sergeant Ramirez and said, "Like what you just gave me, so thank you for that."

He slightly bowed. "My pleasure, ma'am," and left to attend to his duties.

After taking a sip or two of my tea, Jack asked me, "So, will we make it to the outside world today?"

I looked at him, giving him a slight smile. "I think so."

"Yes!"

He's been by my side since everything happened, obviously, but I know he's been worried about my mental state, so him being happy that I'm *finally* getting out of the cabin is a good thing. Even my boys were thrilled as I'm sure they were just as concerned.

Jack asked, "What would you like to do?"

I thought for a moment. "Well, we are in need of some groceries."

Roman remarked, "Yeah, we definitely need chips and cookies."

We all looked at him. I said, "So you're the one who finished my Oreos?!"

He stood straight up as his face screamed, "Oh, shit! I just ratted myself out!" He looked at his wrist at an invisible watch and said, "Woah, would you look at the time." He jogged away.

I shouted, "You ass, I need those cookies right now!"

As he rushed out the door, he said, "Sorry, can't talk right now. Got some important stuff to do."

We all laughed out loud. He's such an asshole, but lord help me, he's *my* asshole!

Jack realized, "And actually, I am in need of some clothes, so …" I looked at him, baffled. He explained, "Some of my clothes ripped that day from being held back by the guys."

My eyes widened. "Oh, no, babe. I'm …"

"No, no, don't you be apologizing. You did nothing wrong, babe." He caressed my face. I melted.

Glen said, "Yeah, I'm surprised you don't have a separated shoulder or anything."

"Oh, trust me, I was hurting a few days ago. It doesn't hurt as much now. It's still a little sore, but I can move it," he said as he demonstrated while wincing a little in pain.

I gently rubbed that shoulder. "Aw, my poor man. Why

didn't you say anything?"

"After what you went through, I was then going to tell you what happened to me? I don't think so. Plus, for you, I don't care if I lost both of my arms that day, I still would've fought for you."

My heart leapt. We stared into each other's eyes with so much love gleaming out of them. He caressed my cheek. From behind me, we heard, "I think I'm going to throw up."

We both glared at Glen for ruining the moment. Glen said, "I'm sorry, guys, but this is a bit much for me," and left.

Kaden was right behind him, saying, "Yeah, sorry, guys. You two are adorable, but … damn. You're making me miss and want Charlie."

We laughed. We then looked back at each other. Jack asked, "Do you want to get ready, and we'll go into town together?"

"You mean like a date?"

He shined as bright as the sun. "Like a date."

"Yay!" I threw my hands up and wrapped my arms around him.

A date! Something we haven't done in a long time!

I chugged my tea, we got dressed, and, with permission from Sergeant Major O'Hare, went into town. Sergeant Major was actually happy for me, as well. "I think that's a great idea, Ms. Ashlynn. Get out for a little bit." But then he became somber and reminded us, "If you see anything, you let me know immediately."

I almost saluted him and said, "Aye, sir," since I was in such a good mood, but then I thought better of it. I instead nodded and replied, "Will do, sir."

I was kind of surprised he didn't have a couple of his

soldiers escort us, but I realized that would technically "cause a scene."

Within minutes, we were in Nonoma. Jack parked the car and as we got out, I looked over and saw the sheriff's office; that beautiful, old Victorian courthouse, which was converted into his office and living quarters. I gawked at it for a second, remembering the day I finally found my brothers.

Jack came around the car and noticed my expression. He looked over and then back at me. "You wanna go in?"

I broke my gaze off the building and looked at him. "I don't know. It's filled with good and bad memories."

He came over and placed his arm around my shoulders. "We should at least meet the new sheriff. He is a fan of the show after all."

We both chuckled. I nodded. "All right, let's go over," and began walking toward it.

The first thing I saw as we got closer were the new front double doors. I had a flashback of when Glen burst through, breaking them off their hinges. I shuddered.

"Baby, you okay?"

"Yeah, I just remembered Glen's 'excessive' entrance."

He waited a moment before asking, "You sure you wanna do this?"

I took a deep breath in, released it, and nodded. He opened the door and let me go first. Entering the sheriff's office brought a wave of memories, a wave of emotions. The white counter was still there with the sheriff's desk not too far behind it. For a second, I saw a flash of Mr. MacReedy sitting there, smiling as we entered. I was then startled back to the present when I heard someone ask, "Can I help you?"

I looked around and noticed another desk to the left with

an older woman sitting at it. She was looking at us somewhat annoyed and confused.

I stepped forward. "Yes, I'm sorry to kind of barge in like this, but we were hoping to see Sheriff O'Neill."

She glowered at us. "Do you have an appointment?"

"No. My name is Ash …"

"Mrs. Graives, what a pleasant surprise!" We looked over and saw a young man dressed in a sheriff's uniform coming toward us. *Damn! Kaden wasn't kidding! This guy is hot!* "It's nice to see you in person."

I smiled. "Yes, sir, it's nice to see you, too."

He came around the counter and walked over to us. He said, "The last time we talked, I know you mentioned making a return trip here, but I didn't think it would be this soon."

I shrugged. "I guess you can say I couldn't wait to get back here."

He laughed and looked over at Jack. "And Mr. Graives, it's truly such an honor." He stuck out his hand and Jack shook it. "I've been watching your show since the very beginning, and I think it's absolutely fascinating."

"Oh, thank you!" They let go of each other's hands. "And please, call me Jack."

Sheriff O'Neill was awestruck. "Well, Jack and …"

"Ashlynn," I gently remarked.

He smiled. "Ashlynn, how can I help you?"

I answered, "Well, we first wanted to stop in and meet you, but we also just wanted to look around, if that's okay."

"We heard this place was ransacked about two years ago by the creatures," Jack interjected.

"Yes, it was. Those doors," pointing to the front doors we just entered, "were torn off the hinges."

We both acted shocked. "Really?!" I asked.

The sheriff nodded. "Yeah. I'm kind of surprised you guys missed this place. Weren't you still in the area?"

We looked at each other. Thank God Jack is quick on his feet, though. He panned back to the sheriff and replied, "I think we were gone already, but that's why we're here now. We would love if you could give us a tour and explain what happened."

"Without your cameras?"

Jesus, this guy is good! But my man is better!

"Well, we didn't want to bombard you with the cameras, sir. And not to sound rude, but we want to make sure it's worth our while. I don't need the execs down my throat saying parts are boring."

Thankfully, Sheriff O'Neill understood. "Makes sense. Please, follow me."

He took us around, explaining what happened in certain areas. It wasn't my boys, but apparently the sheriff's office was ravaged at some point–possibly not too long after we were there. I remember Roman telling me he went back to see if he could find Mr. MacReedy and instead found the place just as bad as they left the lab. The only destruction they did was the front doors. I wouldn't be a bit surprised if Cillian was behind it.

As we went around, we came to the holding cell Jack and the crew were in when I figured out it was Glen who busted through the doors. I grabbed the bars, reliving that memory. I heard Jack when he was begging me to stay instead of going to see who the creature was. *Please, Ashlynn, don't go! You thought the same thing last night and look what happened.*

I looked down at my ankle, which, fortunately, hasn't

been bothering me. That's when I heard, "Ashlynn?" I snapped out of it and looked over at Sheriff O'Neill. "Is everything okay?"

"Oh, yeah, sorry. Just recalling some memories from my youth." Both Jack and Sheriff O'Neill stared at me like I had a thousand heads. "What? The former sheriff and I didn't *always* see eye to eye. Before we got close, there were a few times I was in this cell."

The sheriff looked at me with incredulous eyes. "I doubt that, Ashlynn, but, at the same time, not totally shocked."

We all laughed. We walked around a little more before Sheriff O'Neill looked at his watch and said, "Oh, please forgive me, Jack and Ashlynn, but I have an appointment to get to."

I replied, "It's okay, Sheriff. We actually have some shopping to do."

"So then can we resume this tour on a different day? Maybe with your cameras?" the sheriff inquired.

Jack grinned. "I will talk to my producer and see what we can do."

"Great. Ashlynn, you have my number. If you guys need anything, just shout."

I said, "We will. Thank you so much, Sheriff. And it was truly a pleasure to meet you in person."

"Pleasure was all mine." He shook our hands, and we all left the building.

Jack and I began walking toward the grocery store. He leaned into me and whispered, "'Just recalling memories from my youth?' That's what you came up with?"

I looked at him. "Hey, it worked."

He laughed. "Well, I guess now we *have* to get the crew

out here. Don't want to disappoint the new sheriff."

"Yeah, definitely don't want to do that, especially since he's like our number one fan."

We reached the entrance of the grocery store and Jack leered. He *hates* grocery shopping. I said to him, "Why don't you run to the clothing store, grab some clothes, and meet me here? There's not much I need to get, so neither of us should be long. And then we'll have the rest of the day to ourselves. We can do whatever we want," as I took hold of his hands, interlocking our fingers.

"Are you sure, babe? I mean, what if …"

I looked away, not wanting to think about that possibility. Jack sighed. "I'm sorry, hon." I looked back up at him. "I just … I *can't* lose you again."

"I know, babe." I placed a hand on his cheek and caressed it, putting on the bravest face I could. "But I'll be fine. We haven't heard a peep from Cillian in days. He's probably nursing his wounds and I don't think even *he* can heal that quickly. Plus, you're right across the street." He turned to look at the store front and then back at me. "I promise I won't be long. You, on the other hand."

"Hey, I'm very particular about my clothes."

We both laughed. He gave me a kiss and said, "Don't be long, my love."

"I won't."

He went across the street while I strolled into the grocery store. As I walked in, I saw Charlie working in the produce section. *Oh, yay! I haven't seen him in a while! We need to catch up!*

I walked over to him. "Hey, Charlie!"

He looked over and smiled. "Ashlynn!" He put down the box of lettuce he was working on, wiped his hands on his apron, and came over to give me a big bear hug. I reciprocated. He said, "Oh, honey, it's so good to see you! How are you?"

"I'm well." We let go. "How are you?"

He looked down at the box of lettuce. "Busy working."

I chuckled. "Yeah, I hear ya on that."

He looked back up at me. "So, what brings you back to our apparent monster-infested part of the world."

"Ironically, work."

We both laughed. Then his eyes widened. "Oh, that's right. Kaden told me you got a new job working with your husband, the monster-hunting guy."

My smile disappeared. "Wait, what do you mean Kaden told you?"

He became bashful. He looked down, but I could tell he was beaming as his cheeks turned bright red. "We've been talking. Well, more like texting."

I smirked. *Kaden, you sly dog!* I said, "Aw, good, I'm glad."

He waited a moment before he said, "I know."

I looked at him, perplexed. "You know …?"

He glared at me. "Ashlynn, I know."

That's when it hit me. "Oh, you mean …"

"Yup."

"Wait … how?"

"I made him show me."

I couldn't help but laugh. "I'm sorry, did you say you *made* him show you what he looks like now?"

Smiling, he nodded. "I told him I really wanted to see him and that I missed him. He fought me for some time, but he eventually caved, and I met him by the movie theater." He paused.

"And?!" I was getting antsy. I wanted to hear more. I was kind of excited knowing I'm not the only one (other than Jack and our crew … and my parents … and Mr. Scarlo) who knows about them now.

He continued, "At first, I hate to say it, but I was a little scared. I mean there's my boyfriend …"

"Boyfriend?!"

He twinkled and nodded. I hugged him. "Oh my gosh, I'm so happy to hear!"

I'm going to kill Kaden for not telling me!

"Thank you, honey!" We let go of each other. "So, anyway, yeah, there's my boyfriend looking *totally* different from when I first met him, but literally seconds later I was fine. I went over to him and gave him a hug and a kiss."

I placed my hand over my heart. "Aw, really?!"

"Yeah, girl. That's my man!"

I died. "I love you, Charlie. You're the best." He laughed. "What did Kaden do when you did that?"

"He was actually a little upset with me, but I told him to get over it." I laughed again. "But yeah, we've been seeing each other here and there since then, but we definitely text each other every day; especially in the morning and at night."

"Aw, you guys are too cute."

He shrugged and then looked at me with excitement. "Let's take a selfie and I'll send it to him."

I replied with so much joy, "Yes!" *God I so needed this!*

We took the selfie. He sent it over to Kaden. "Oh, I can't wait to see what he says."

I giggled. "Me, too."

"Okay, honey, I'm sorry, I don't want to be rude, but I need to get back to work."

"Oh my gosh, no worries! It was so great seeing you. Maybe we can do a double date at the cabin soon?"

His eyes lit up. "Yas, girl! I would love that!"

"Awesome. I'll talk to Kaden, and we'll get something figured out."

"Sounds good, sweetie. See you later."

He went back to work while I started shopping. But moments later, he came over to me, got close to me, and whispered, "Ashlynn, I think you need to get out of here."

"What? What are you talking about?"

"Kaden just answered me. He said he's so happy to see a smile on your face because you've been through some stuff. And when I asked him to explain, he said some guy has been after you. Honey, what if that guy is here?"

I let out the breath I was holding. "Oh, Charlie, you just gave me such a scare." He glared at me, confused. "I thought I was being tossed out."

"Oh, no, sweetie, never. But seriously, what if that guy is here?"

"Charlie, if he was, trust me, you would know it."

All of a sudden, we (and everyone else in the store) heard—and felt—a loud bang come from the back wall. We jumped and looked over. "What the hell was that?" Charlie asked.

My cheery demeanor immediately left my body. My heart stopped. The smile on my face disappeared. I felt my color drain. I pushed out, "The guy who's after me," as I looked back at Charlie. He looked at me, his eyes screaming with confusion and fear.

Seconds later, there was another bang, and then another that echoed throughout the store, but this time we also heard rock crumbling. *Fuck, that's not good!*

Finally, there was another hit, succeeded by an explosive bang and a fist popping through the wall. "Shit!"

People started screaming and running. I turned to Charlie and shouted, "Get these people out of here! Call Kaden and tell him Cillian's here! Tell him to get Sergeant Major O'Hare and his troops here immediately!"

He nodded frantically. "What are you going to do?"

Cillian punched again and now his whole arm came through. "Distract him." I panned back to Charlie, slightly pushed him, and ordered, "Go! Now!"

He ran, gathering people and herding them toward the entrance. I turned back and saw a hole in the wall. Then I saw those damn fire-ember eyes. They smiled. He stood, wound up, and punched again, making the hole bigger. "All right, Ashlynn, it's time to face your fear," I said, my voice trembling and my body quivering.

As he pulled back, he grabbed the wall to make the hole even bigger. He looked in. "I found you, my love."

Shaking, I outstretched my arms and said, "You want me, asshole." He smirked. "Come find me."

I turned and ran. I tried to think as quickly as possible where to hide and I just ducked down an aisle in the nick of time as Cillian broke through. I stopped dead in my tracks, crouched down, and tried not to breathe, so he wouldn't find me. I could hear–and feel on the floor–him starting to walk toward where I was. He said, "You may be able to run, my love, but you can't hide from me. I can hear you breathing; I can hear your heart racing." He took a loud breath in. "And I can smell you. So delectable."

God you're disgusting!

As I stayed in my crouching position, I crab-walked backwards, keeping an eye at the end of the aisle to make sure he didn't see me. I also kept on looking around to make sure he wasn't coming from a different direction. The moment I saw his foot, I was able to scurry over and out of sight. He kept on walking, going down the aisle I just came from. He chuckled. "I can see your shadow."

I looked over to my left and saw it, too. "Shit!" I got up and ran as he thudded down the aisle. Luckily, the shelves were taller than him, so he couldn't see where I was going. I was able to, once again, duck behind a produce display just in time. He growled and bellowed, "I will get you and you will be mine, Ashlynn!"

That's when I glanced over to my right and saw two kids (one probably around eleven and the other around seven, older boy and younger girl) hiding behind another produce display. They were absolutely terrified and crying.

Oh, no!

They sniffled. I immediately placed an index finger over my lips and mouthed, "It's going to be okay. I will get you out of here."

They nodded.

My mind raced as I tried to think of a way to distract him, so I could get the kids out. I peeked around the corner to see what he was doing. I saw his back was to us. I noticed the apples above my head. I grabbed one, stood up, and threw it as hard as I could toward the other side of the store. I crouched back down and heard him run toward it. I quickly crawled over to the kids and whispered. "Are you guys okay?" They nodded. "Good. Stay close to me. We're going to get out of here, okay?" They nodded again and grabbed ahold of my hands.

We started running toward the entrance only to be stopped by Cillian jumping right in front of us. I placed them behind me. He inquired, "Where do you think you're going?"

"I'm getting them out of here, Cillian! They're innocent children! Let them go!" He growled. Then I thought of something that made me physically ill. "Let them go and I'll do whatever you want."

He grinned from ear to ear. "Fine, but don't try anything funny."

I kept the kids behind me as we went around him. I brought them over to the door, knelt in front of them, and looked at them. The little girl was trembling, tears streaming down her rosy cheeks. The boy was trying to put on a courageous front, but he was just as scared. My heart sank. "Hey, it's going to be okay," I said as I gently rubbed their arms. They looked up at him and shivered some more. "Don't look at him, keep your eyes on me, okay?" They did as I said. "My name is Ashlynn. What are yours?"

The little girl said, "Sophie" and the boy said, "Brandon."

"Brandon, Sophie, you guys have been so brave. Now, go outside and find your parents or an adult, okay?"

Sophie whimpered, "But I don't want to leave you with the monster."

Cillian snarled behind me. I actually felt some anger rage inside me when he did that. I wanted to turn around and tell him to fuck off, but I kept my composure, softly grabbed Sophie's shoulders, and said, "I will be fine, sweetie. Now go!" I somewhat forcibly turned them and pushed them toward the door.

They ran out, screaming, "Mommy! Mommy!"

Thankfully, I heard a woman yell, "Sophie! Brandon!" before Cillian quipped, "Aw, how motherly of you."

I was about to turn around and say something when I saw Jack being held back by some soldiers. I thought I was far enough away from Cillian that I could make a run for it, but I forgot his reach. I screamed for Jack and tried darting to him, but Cillian grabbed me by the back of my neck and pulled me in, hollering, "Come here!" He made me face him. "You're mine now!"

I looked straight into his dead eyes and said, "Sophie's right, you *are* a fucking monster."

He growled, baring his teeth, and grabbed me around my neck. Again, he wasn't choking me, but just holding me. I grabbed his wrist. He pulled me into him. "I am *not* a monster! I am a *fucking GOD!*"

He pushed me down so hard that I actually skidded across the floor a few feet. When I stopped, I stayed in position for a second, racked in pain. Then I heard—and felt—his footsteps coming toward me. I looked up to see him strutting my way. "It's time to make good on your promise."

That's when I heard someone running toward us. I looked over and saw one of my boys charging at Cillian. "Glen!" I hollered.

He jumped over me and tackled Cillian down with a thunderous crash. He got up and waited for Cillian to make a move, but he actually stayed down. *Damn! Glen must've hit him pretty hard for him to not immediately get up and fight back!*

He came over to me and helped me up. "You okay, Ash?"

"Much better, now that you're here." We smiled at each other.

"Aw," Cillian said as he slowly got up, coughing. "How

sweet. Little brother trying to rescue his big sister."

"Who said anything about trying, asshole?" he said, placing me behind him.

Cillian was about to do something when Sergeant Major and his troops burst into the store, pointing their guns at him. "It's over, Cillian!"

"Ha! That's what you think, O'Hare. It's only just beginning."

"Don't do anything stupid."

"Or what? What will you do? Shoot me?"

"We now know your weakness, Cillian. We can, and we will, kill you."

Cillian roared with laughter. "You mean that little hole you opened up?" He pointed to where he got injured the other night. "Do you see any scars?" We all looked and saw nothing.

"Jesus!" I exclaimed.

"When will it get through your thick skulls that I AM A FUCKING GOD!"

We all continued to stare at him, the soldiers' guns steady on him. He panned over to me, held out his hand, and said, "Come, my love."

I shook my head, holding onto Glen's arm as he gripped me tighter. From behind the soldiers, Jack came forward and shouted, "She doesn't belong to you, Cillian."

Cillian looked at him and *tsk-tsked* him. "That's where you're wrong Jackie-boy. She IS mine!"

Glen roared and stampeded toward him. I yelled, "No, Glen!" He tossed Cillian into the wall and threw punch after punch.

Suddenly, I felt arms wrap around me. I looked over to see my man. "Jack!" I wrapped my arms around him. He pulled me over to the soldiers. The second we were behind them, Sergeant Major commanded, "Fire!"

"No!" I shouted as they began shooting. "Glen, watch out!"

He got hit a couple of times but was able to duck to let the continuous rounds hit Cillian. "Aim for one area!" Sergeant Major ordered.

"Aim for his neck!" I added, hoping they would get his jugular and the son of a bitch would bleed out. Seconds later, they did open up a wound, but it was closer to his shoulder than his neck. He roared and ran off through the hole he had created. As soon as he was outside, I saw two creatures try to attack him—Kaden and Roman—and there were more soldiers waiting for him, but he just plowed through everybody, including my boys, and kept running to the woods. Roman and Kaden followed him, plus Sergeant Major sent a few of his soldiers to track any blood trail he might've left behind.

With Jack's arms already wrapped around me, I grabbed him and held him closer. He kissed the top of my head, muttering, "Thank you, thank you."

Glen came over to us. I let go of my husband and embraced my brother. He reciprocated. I said, "I truly have the best brother in the world."

"Hey, nobody messes with my sister." I hugged him tighter. "By the way, can I get a recording of that?"

I smacked him as we laughed. "Hell, you can record me, and I'll post it all over social media."

"Yes!"

We let go of each other. Sergeant Major walked over. He asked, "Are you okay, Ms. Ashlynn?"

"I am. Thank you for saving my life once again, Sergeant

Major."

"My pleasure."

I surveyed the store, taking in the destruction caused by this maniacal monster. "Sergeant Major." He looked at me. "We need to do something about Cillian, and fast. He's going to continue this path of destruction until ..."

Sergeant Major stopped me. "Don't finish that sentence, Ms. Ashlynn."

"But it's true, Sergeant Major." I didn't want to say this in front of my husband or my brother, but I came to a grave conclusion. With a massive knot in my stomach, I said, "Maybe I should just give myself to him. It'll save ..."

All three men echoed, "NO!"

Sergeant Major snapped, "Absolutely not, Ashlynn! Don't talk like that! He and his goons were destroying buildings before ..."

"To draw me in!" I interjected.

Sergeant Major and Jack were flabbergasted. Glen snapped, "I fucking knew it!"

Jack inquired, "What do you mean, babe? How do you know?"

"I didn't tell you, but when he kidnapped me, he revealed how all he wanted to do was be with me after hearing you guys," pointing to Glen, "talk about me. What better way to get me back here than by attacking my second home?"

You saw the realization hit Jack and Sergeant Major like they ran into a brick wall. Glen, however, was upset and hurt. "We should've known better than to talk about you around those guys. But we were so worried about you. We hoped and prayed you were safe."

I gently grabbed his arm and said, "Don't think for one

second you guys are to blame for this. You did nothing wrong. Cillian and his massive fucking ego are to blame."

Sergeant Major stepped in. "Well, you're not giving yourself up to that maniac. We may have a solution." I looked at him, somewhat confused. "Please come with me, Ms. Ashlynn. You, too, Glen. Meet us there."

"Meet you where?" I inquired.

"The white building."

My heart sank. *No! Please, not that fucking place!*

Glen nodded his head. He looked at me. "I'll find Roman and Kaden and meet you there."

I nodded. "Sounds good," and he left.

Jack spoke up, "Uh, what about me?"

Sergeant Major answered, "No offense, Mr. Graives, but I'm going to ask you to go back to the cabin."

Jack became defensive. "Hell no! I'm not leaving my wife alone when that asshole is still running around!"

Before Sergeant Major could say anything and start a war in the middle of a dilapidated grocery store, I said, "I won't be alone, Jack. I'll be surrounded by the soldiers and my brothers will be there, as well."

He continued boring a hole into Sergeant Major O'Hare, like he was about to pounce on him. I asked him, "Do you trust me?"

He looked down at me, his anger slowly melting. "Of course, I do. But the last time you asked me that question, you came back to me with a bleeding, fractured ankle."

I gave him a half smile. "True, but I was also by myself. This time I won't be. Here's a better question, then, do you trust my brothers?"

Without any hesitation, he answered, "Yes."

"Then know I will come back to you."

Our foreheads met. "You better."

I kissed him. Sergeant Major cleared his throat. We looked at him. "My apologies, Ms. Ashlynn, but like you said, we need to do something about Cillian, so please, come with me."

He escorted Jack and me out of the store. There was a slew of people standing around the entrance, being held back by soldiers, with their phones out. *Oh, great! I'm sure Mr. Robinson will love this!*

But then a few soldiers surrounded us, so we weren't seen. However, Sophie and Brandon saw me. They came running over, screaming, "Ashlynn! Ashlynn!"

The one soldier in front of me moved, so I could kneel down. They ran into my arms, crying. Sophie wailed, "I was so scared for you. Are you okay?"

I held them tight. "Yes, sweetie, I'm fine."

They let go of me and I held them at arm's length. Brandon asked, "Is the monster gone?"

I nodded. "For now."

"We heard gunshots and fighting. Is he dead?" sweet, little Sophie asked.

"I don't think so." Fear flared up in her reddened eyes. "But I am working with my friend here, Sergeant Major O'Hare," I looked at him and he actually bent down to look at the two kids, "and we may have a solution."

"Wow!" they exclaimed.

Brandon inquired, "Are you really in the army?"

Sergeant Major smiled. "I am."

"Cool!"

I grinned. *Typical boy!*

Then a woman, probably a little older than me, came over. I stood up. She walked over to me and gave me a tight hug. I, of course, reciprocated. She cried, "Thank you for saving my babies."

"It was my pleasure." We let go of each other. "You've raised two amazing and brave kids."

"Thank you! How can I ever repay you?"

Jack, who was standing behind me and placed his hand on my shoulder. "Just … keep on raising them right."

She smiled. Sophie asked, "Will I ever see you again?"

"I don't know, sweetie. But if it's okay with your mom, I would love to check in on you guys and make sure you're okay."

Their mother answered, "Absolutely! We would really appreciate that!"

We exchanged numbers, hugged one more time, and went our separate ways.

Still being surrounded by soldiers, I walked Jack to the car. He said, "Well, that just proved to me that you'll be an amazing mom."

I chuckled. "Yeah, well, you need to put a baby in me first, Mr. Graives."

He leaned in and whispered, "We'll continue working on that once this whole ordeal is over."

We locked eyes. "Promise?"

He winked. "Promise."

I gave him one last kiss before he got in the car and drove off.

****

On the car ride, Sergeant Major asked, "Do you and Jack have any kids?"

I rubbed my tummy. "No, not yet."

"Well, I can tell you'll be an amazing mom when the time comes."

I beamed. "Thank you, sir. And you? Do you have any kids?"

"Oh, yes. And grandkids around the same age as the ones you saved."

I was kind of shocked. He doesn't seem old enough to be a grandfather. He clarified, "My wife and I started young. We were in love, so …"

I put my hand up. "No need to explain yourself, sir."

He smirked and looked away.

Like with Sergeant Ramirez, I had to ask, "Why this job, Sergeant Major?"

He groaned, not in disgust or misery, though. "I was waiting for you to ask me that." I released a small chuckle. "Ms. Ashlynn, there's no motive or anything like that, unlike our 'friend,' Mr. MacReedy." I cringed when he said his name. "I'm sorry to say, but it's just a job. Like I said, I have a wife, kids, and grandkids back home. I need to take care of them, provide for them. Trust me, I'd rather be home with them, but," he put his hands up, "you unfortunately have to do what you are told, no questions asked."

As much as I didn't like it, believe it or not, I understood and my respect for him grew.

Pulling up to what I guess was the entrance to this hell hole, I saw my boys waiting. The second the car stopped, I jumped out and ran into Kaden's arms.

"Glad to see you're okay, hon."

"I'm glad you guys are okay, too." I let go of him and went over to Roman. As we let go of each other, Sergeant

Major said, "Please, follow me. I have something I need to show you."

We entered the building, shadowing Sergeant Major, going into an elevator that brought us down several levels. The doors opened to a large white room. No, literally *everything* was white, from the ceiling down to the floor. Ahead of us were some workers talking, some soldiers standing guard, and smaller rooms with what looked like floor to ceiling glass doors. They kind of looked like interrogation rooms, just without the table and chairs. There were two rooms in front of us and two on either side. I asked, "What are those for?"

Sergeant Major replied, "They're safety rooms. The doors are made of polycarbonate glass and can only be accessed by a special code. The walls are made of steel and concrete. We created them to keep the creatures in if we ever caught one alive."

"Or keep them out?"

He looked at me. "Or keep them out."

We continued walking toward a hall that was off to the right of the rooms in front of us. He came to a door. He knocked on it and it opened. An unenthusiastic voice asked, "Yes, Sergeant Major, how can I help you?"

Oh, that voice sounds familiar!

I looked in and saw a person standing at the door. "Dr. Park?!"

He looked up from his clipboard. "Ashlynn!" he exclaimed, smiling. "This is a pleasant surprise. Please, come in."

We all walked in. I gawked at him. I didn't know what to make of this, so I said, "Yeah, it's definitely a surprise. Are you ..."

Before I finished, he replied, "I am, but," he put his hands up, still holding onto his clipboard and pen, "I was not the one who made the original serum. He's long gone. I am, however, helping to find a 'cure,' if you will."

The boys shouted unanimously, "A cure?!"

I jumped a little and covered my ears since they did that right in them. "Ow, shit!"

"Oh, sorry, hon," Kaden said, placing a hand on my shoulder.

Dr. Park looked at them. "Yes. I've been working on a way to make any and all creatures revert back to being ..."

"Human," Roman finished for him.

"Exactly."

I was a little befuddled. "Wait a minute, Dr. Park. I thought you were a 'regular' physician."

He laughed a little. "I am, but I also studied microbiology, biochemistry, and regular chemistry, among other fields."

I asked, somewhat sarcastically, "Why? For shits and giggles?"

"Ha! No, my two goals in life were to become a doctor and work on a cure for a disease, mainly cancer. I may be doing this a little earlier than I wanted, and it may not be cancer, but I'm happy to be helping."

I was impressed. Then Kaden inquired, "Any luck with a cure for us?"

"Well, kind of. I've been working with lab rats, giving them the serum, waiting for them to turn, and then giving them 'the cure' and ..."

"And?!" my boys almost yelled.

I let out an angry sigh since they shouted in my ears again.

"They've been changing back, but with one major side effect."

Now I joined them. "Which is?!" We were all on the edge of our seats. Well, feet since we were standing.

"Death."

My heart sank and I could tell the boys were disappointed. Dr. Park continued, "I don't know why, but they all have died. Some of them I've been able to revive, but not all. I feel like there's either too much or too little of something somewhere, but I can't pinpoint it."

I asked, "Are you close to pinpointing what this factor could be?"

His face was sullen. "No, unfortunately not."

Shit!

Then my mind drifted back for a moment. "Wait, you mentioned you used the serum on the rats and *waited* for them to change. Did you torture them at all?"

His eyes widened and he looked at Sergeant Major O'Hare. "You didn't tell her?"

The Sergeant Major's face screamed, "Ah, shit!"

I gaped at him. "Didn't tell me what?"

Sergeant Major hesitantly began, "We knew which serum turned people and which one didn't. The 'torture,' as you put it, was just to speed up the process, or at least that's what we were told. At first, we deemed anybody who changed as a 'failure' but realized we actually wanted them." He looked at my boys. "You guys blend in more with the environment. *You're* the super soldiers we wanted."

Kaden interjected, "Wait a minute … What was your process for choosing who got which serum?"

Once again, Sergeant Major hesitantly replied, "We didn't have one. It was like Russian Roulette, we just grabbed and whichever one we grabbed, you got."

I was boiling over with fury. I hollered, "And now, because of that, there's a fucking monster running around who thinks he's a fucking god!"

My boys put their hands on my shoulders, and someone grabbed my arm to hold me back. I was ready to pounce on him and beat him to a bloody pulp. I didn't care if I would be put in jail for the rest of my life, I was *fucking* angry!

Sergeant Major continued, "It wasn't until everyone escaped that we realized our error and did whatever we could to rectify that mistake."

"So you killed most before it registered, 'Hey, maybe we can make a cure and save these guys?'"

He looked at me, then looked down, sighed, and nodded.

The guys now really had to grab me. "You son of a bitch! So this is just a job, huh?!"

He looked back up at me, his eyes drilling into me. I didn't flinch, I was not scared one bit of what he was about to say or do. "I'll let that one slide because I understand you're upset, but you better watch what you say! Don't forget who the hell I am!"

"Yeah, the ass …"

"Ashlynn, stop!" Kaden shouted.

"What?!"

"Look, I'm not happy with what I'm hearing either, but it's not worth getting yourself into trouble!"

I took several deep breaths in. I began to calm down, but only a little bit. Sergeant Major regained his composure, as well. "Now, I know apologizing won't do any good."

"Damn, right!" I stated.

"But I do hope bringing you here and this possible cure is a step in the right direction."

I cooled down a little more, to the point where even the guys felt they could let go of me. I replied, "A tiny step."

He gave me a slight bow. "I'll take it. Now, I'll give you all some privacy with Dr. Park. Let's figure out a way to get Cillian."

I nodded. Sergeant Major O' Hare opened the door, walked out, and closed it behind him. I waited a few seconds before saying, "It's a good thing you guys stopped me, or I would be in the fucking brig for punching a sergeant major in the face."

Roman chimed in, "And I would be right next to you for cheering you on. Maybe even throwing a few myself."

We all laughed. I looked over at Dr. Park, who wasn't amused. I cleared my throat. "Please forgive me, Dr. Park. I didn't …"

He put up his hand to stop me. "No need to explain yourself, Ashlynn. I do understand where you're coming from. I will admit, I felt the same way when I found out, but knew it was way more important to find a cure. Let's now work together to put an end to this horrible nightmare."

I smiled. "I couldn't agree more."

Then Roman asked, "Dr. Park, would you be willing to test this new serum on a person?"

He looked at him. "Son, I know the prospect of being 'normal' again is extremely enticing, but I am not comfortable with injecting any of you with it, especially with the possibility of death."

They looked at each other. I watched them. I knew exactly what they were thinking. "No."

They panned over to me. Kaden started walking over to me. "Ashlynn."

I repeated, shaking my head, "No!"

He reached me and grasped my shoulders. "Honey, we need to see. We need to know if this can work on us and not just on a lab rat."

"No! Absolutely not! I am not losing any of you! I would rather inject Cillian with it, and *he* possibly dies than any of you!"

Roman tried chiming in, "Ashlynn, we …"

I continued my rant. "No! You're not testing this 'cure' on yourselves!" Tears rolled down my cheeks. The room fell silent for a moment.

Glen came over to me, wrapped his arms around me, and said, "Ashlynn, we need to know if it works. If it does turn one of us back, then we just may have a chance against Cillian."

"But how?" I sobbed.

Kaden explained, "Two of us can weaken him enough so the other can inject him and turn him back."

"But …"

"Hey." Glen loosened his grip so I could look up at him. "I'm not going to lose my sister to this monster when there's a possibility I can do something about it."

I cried more and fell back into his chest. However, after a moment, Dr. Park said, "I'm truly sorry, everyone, but I have some bad news to share." We all looked at him. "I've been wondering why Cillian is so much bigger and so much stronger than everyone else. I looked into his file and learned that he wasn't injected once with the serum, but at least twice."

My eyes widened, lifting myself up off Glen. "What?!"

He nodded. "They 'saw something in him' and decided

to see what would happen if someone was injected more than once, and well … we got a true monster on our hands."

We all became furious. "What the …"

"But wait, there's more."

We all shouted at once, "More?!"

"I injected a lab rat twice with the serum and then, after some time, with the 'cure.'"

Oh, Jesus Christ, man! "And?!"

"Nothing. It didn't die, it didn't change back, there was no reaction. I even injected it at least one other time, with a stronger dosage, and nothing. It's like doubling up on the serum made it immune."

"No!" I literally screamed out, falling back into Glen.

"Shit!" Roman exclaimed.

"Then what do we do, Dr. Park?" Kaden asked, trying to be the calm and logical one in the group.

"The only thing I can think of is capturing him, so I can study him. Maybe he's the true answer to this cure."

Roman stated, "Hell no, Doc! This asshole needs to fucking die! Do you know what he's tried to do to Ashlynn?"

Dr. Park looked down. "I don't, but I saw in his file that he's a convicted stalker and rapist …"

"Oh, Jesus!" I screamed.

"… so, unfortunately, I can only imagine. I'm truly sorry, Ashlynn."

Roman continued his tirade, "And how the fuck are we supposed to capture a monster?"

Dr. Park looked defeated. "I don't know."

A second later, Kaden said, "I do." We looked at him as he looked at us. "We become as strong as him."

I straightened up, letting go of Glen. "You're not saying,

Kaden …"

"Yes, I am. We have to, hon. At this point, there's no other way."

God damnit! I didn't want to admit it, but he was right. I rubbed my forehead. "This is truly a fucking nightmare."

Dr. Park sounded off, "I'm sorry, Ashlynn, but I actually agree with him. It's our best plan right now. If we knew Cillian was away and wouldn't return for some time, then we could use that to our advantage and come up with something better. But that's not the case. He may be right outside this building as we speak."

I remembered, "Well, the last time he got hit by bullets and bled, we didn't hear from him for a few days. He just got hit again at the store, so he should be wherever he goes to nurse his wounds. We should be fine."

"Ashlynn! Come out here, my love!"

I looked toward the door. My heart raced and my eyes almost popped out of my head. I muttered, "No! You're fucking kidding me, right?!"

Roman became infuriated. "Well, isn't that a fucking coincidence! You mentioned that Cillian may be right outside and here he is! Are you working with him, Doc?" Roman accused in a low voice. I was actually really proud of him for not "giving up our position," if you will. We didn't know if he knew the boys were with me and we didn't want him to run.

"Of course not! But he just proved my point! Now we need to act fast!" Dr. Park whispered.

The boys looked at each other and I looked at them. It took every bit of me to finally say, "Do it!"

Kaden inquired, "Are you sure, hon?"

I shook my head. "But we have no other choice at this

point."

Kaden nodded. "Okay. Dr. Park, do your thing."

He took a deep breath in, let it out, and nodded. He gently put down his clipboard and pen, trying not to make too much noise, and went over to the mini fridge in the corner of the room. He opened it and took out three vials of a clear liquid. Just as he was about to close it, Glen said, "Wait, Dr. Park." He looked at him. "Do you have any more of 'the cure' left?"

"I do." He was a little stumped.

"Take one of those out, please. I have an idea."

I grabbed his arm. "What do you mean you have an idea?"

"Ashlynn! I know you're back there! I have a present for you, my love!"

I became extremely nauseous. Glen asked, "Do you trust me?"

I was stunned by the question. "Of course, I do!"

"Then I *severely* hate to say this but get out there before he comes back here. We will not be too far behind you."

I panned around him to see Roman and Kaden agreeing. "Fine, but I better see *all* of you *really* soon!"

He smiled. "You will, sis."

I hugged him. "I love you, Glen."

"I love you, too, Ash."

I went over and hugged Roman and Kaden before we heard an earth-shattering, "ASHLYNN!"

My heart may have been pounding so hard in my chest that it hurt, but I was ready to face him. As I went to let go of Kaden, he held onto my shoulders and said, "You got this, hon."

My lips curled up slightly. I brought my chin up, walked over to the door, opened it, walked out into the corridor, and closed the door behind me. I took another deep breath in and let it out before I began stepping slowly toward the front room. Upon entering it, I saw a circle of soldiers, pointing their guns, surrounding Cillian, his wound nearly gone. But he wasn't alone. I could see he was holding someone, but I couldn't tell who. When our eyes met, he beamed. "My love."

I continued walking in and went over to Sergeant Major O'Hare. I stood next to him and finally saw who was with Cillian. It was Mr. MacReedy. Cillian had his massive paw over his mouth. He was all bloody and bruised. It looked like he had him as his captive for a couple of days. My face fell. My heart dropped through the floor. *Oh, dear god! He warned me and I ignored him!*

"Look what I have for you. We can finally have our revenge."

Mr. MacReedy was trying to say something through Cillian's hand. Cillian shouted, "Shut up!" Mr. MacReedy immediately quieted down.

Sergeant Major ordered, "Let him go, Cillian!"

"Why should I? He might've made me a god, but he took everything away from so many, including my love." He looked at me before returning his gaze back to Sergeant Major. "He deserves to rot in Hell!"

I pleaded, "Please let him go, Cillian! I know there's a part of you that's still human." He glared at me. *Fuck! If looks could kill!* But I stood my ground and continued, "What he did was wrong, but he doesn't deserve to be harmed."

"This coming from the same woman who was ready to kill this bastard only days ago."

Holy shit! He was waiting for him!

I sighed. "Yes, I was angry with him, but Mr. ... Sheriff MacReedy." He looked at me. "I forgive you."

Cillian let him go, staggered by what I said. I was so relieved to see him released from Cillian's grip. Former Sheriff MacReedy looked at me and the look of solace on his face made me smile. He said, "Thank you, darlin'. I am truly so ...'"

Before he could finish his sentence, Cillian placed his hand on top of his head and pushed down, flattening the former sheriff all the way to the floor. His blood and guts sprayed like a sprinkler. It went everywhere, including me. "Too much sentimental bullshit," Cillian said as he stood up.

It took me (and everyone) a hot second to register what had happened, but when it did, I let out a blood-curdling scream. Sergeant Major hollered, "OPEN FIRE," and his troops began shooting at Cillian. The only effect they had on him was they pissed him off. I wanted to shout, "Aim for one spot," but I was in utter shock. I just watched him as he ran around, swatting at each man like they were gnats in his face. Suddenly, Sergeant Major grabbed me, ran me to one of the cells, punched in a security code, threw me in, and immediately closed it and locked it. "You'll be safe in here. I'll come back for you."

I banged my hands on the door. "No! Sergeant Major!"

I was then reminded of the blood and guts on my hands, on my pants, on my shirt, on my face, and in my hair. I continued screaming, turning away from the mayhem, walking away from the door, and frantically rubbing myself all over. I sobbed, doing all I could to get the former sheriff's blood (and whatever else) off me. That's when I realized something that frightened me even more. It was quiet. No gunfire. No orders being shouted. No screams.

I slowly turned to see Cillian standing in front of the cell door. I immediately backed up to a wall. He leered. "Hi, baby."

He placed his blood-soaked hand on the polycarbonate glass door. I jumped, placing my hand over my mouth. "Jesus Christ!"

"No, not Jesus." He pointed to himself. "God!"

Oh, fuck this! With whatever fortitude I had, I pushed myself off the wall and hollered, "Fuck you, Cillian! You're nothing! You're nobody!"

He chuckled. "There's my badass girl I fell in love with."

I marched over to the door and looked him straight in the eyes. "You know what you are?" Looking down at me, he cocked his head to one side and raised an eyebrow. "You're a piece of shit. You have no right to look me in the eyes and tell me you love me because you have no heart and no soul."

"How can you say that after what I did for you?" he asked, turning and pointing at the carnage that was behind him. His "masterpiece," as he saw it.

"You slaughtered innocent people!"

"I served up justice!" he bellowed.

"Justice? That …?" I pointed to the destruction, "that's justice?!"

He sighed. "I see now you don't appreciate my gift, or me, really. I guess it's time to teach you a lesson." He rounded up and punched the device in order to unlock the door, but it didn't work. Then he punched the door with all of his might. I shrieked, covering myself up, expecting glass to spray all over me, but the door held up. Not even a scratch.

He continued pounding on the door for a moment or two

before stopping and examining it. He still barely made any sort of dent in it. I began to laugh uncontrollably. "Oh, what's the matter? The big bad wolf can't break down the door?"

"Oh, honey, you haven't seen what this wolf can do."

I immediately stopped laughing. "Shit!"

He took a few steps back away from the door and then threw himself at it. I jumped. We both looked to see if any damage was done and the son of a bitch did it. He made a crack in it. "Oh, shit!"

He did it again, this time backing up a little further. The crack got bigger. "Fuck!"

He smiled. He backed up again, even further. Just before he leapt into action, he exclaimed, "Don't worry, baby! Daddy's coming!"

I screamed as he charged at the door like a locomotive. Thankfully, just before he was about to hit it, a creature just as big as him jumped him. It started pounding him like they were in a mixed martial arts fight. I ran to the door to try and see who it was. While staring out, another massive creature with darker skin came to the door. "You okay, babe?"

I was floored. "Roman?!" He winked at me. "Holy shit, dude! It worked!"

"I knew it would. Now step back. I'm going to break this down and get you into another room."

I nodded and ran back, covering myself up the best I could. He broke through it easily, which scared me. *If they hadn't stopped him, Cillian would've probably run me over!*

Roman held out his arms. "Come on, babe!"

I ran right into them, and he carried me to another cell. But before we reached it, I felt Roman get hit from behind and we went down, hard. All I felt was pain and all I saw were stars. Roman yelled, "Keep going," as he fought off Cillian.

It took me some time, but I got up and went to take my first step when I felt a sharp pain in my bad ankle. I yelped and fell to the ground, grasping it. "Fuck! Not now!"

Then I felt hands wrap around my waist, gently picking me up. "I got you, sweetie."

I looked over to see my best friend. "Kaden!"

He began helping me over to the cell, but I stopped him. "Go help, Roman. I'll be okay."

"Are you sure?"

"Yes, go."

"Okay, but I'll be right back." He turned to help Roman while I continued toward the cell. Eventually, I reached the door. I went to pull it open only to be reminded it needed a code. "Ah, shit!"

I decided to try "1, 2, 3, 4," which didn't work. "Okay, what about 4, 3, 2, 1."

The light turned green. I laughed. "Yes!"

I opened the door, went in, and tried closing it when a force stopped it. I looked up to see Cillian. I fell into the wall beside me, staring up at him, knowing my fate. He leaned in and caressed my cheek. He got close to my face and said, "Now, I got you."

"Hey!" He was flung away from me, across to the other side of the space, and hit the wall, making a dent in it. "I saw her first, dick!"

Relieved, I said, "God, I love you!"

Roman looked back at me and smirked. "Watch out, hon. I'll close the door and lock you in."

I backed up a little more and Roman tried closing it, but it wouldn't lock. "Oh, come on!" he exclaimed.

"Fuck! Cillian must've broke it when he stopped me."

We heard groans and loud bangs coming from behind him. We looked to see Kaden and Cillian fighting in the background. Roman panned back to me and said, "Get out of here, Ash. We'll hold him off."

"I'm not leaving you guys!"

"Babe, don't even start. We'll do all we can to stop him from getting to you. Now go!"

He turned to go help Kaden. As he did, I yelled, "Roman," but he was already part of the brawl. I went to take a step, and once again, did it on my bad ankle. I fell back into the wall, wincing in pain. I tried to problem-solve as quickly as possible, figuring out how the hell I was going to get out of that space with my bad ankle and where I was going to hide as my boys fought off the brute.

I decided to get down and try to military crawl toward the elevator. My ankle still hurt, but it wasn't as bad as stepping on it. As I inched my way through, trying to get out, I felt something grab my bad ankle and pull me back. I screamed, my nails clawing at the floor, trying to stop my inevitable doom, to only break off a few from the nail bed—that's how hard I was trying. I was then forcibly turned over. I looked up to see that disgusting monster, Cillian. I continued screaming. He laid on top of me. "No! Get off me!"

He began groping every bit of me. I tried fighting back, but he took my hands and held them down, above my head, with just one of his. I knew I was done for. If Roman and Kaden were down, then that was it; I was his. With a shit-eating grin on his face, he continued touching me. He said, "Oh, my love. I've waited so long for this. It's time to have some fun."

I cried, "No! Please stop!"

Then from behind him, we heard, "Hey, asshole!"

Holy shit, another voice that sounds familiar!

He stopped, got up, turned around, and roared, "What now?!"

I sat up and peeked around him. My eyes popped with joy. "Get away from my sister!"

I exclaimed in a higher pitch than normal, "Glen!"

He raised the weapon he picked up (looked like an AK-47) and began shooting at Cillian to get him away from me. I continued staring at my brother because he looked like himself again. I couldn't believe it. He looked over at me and shouted, "Get out of here, Ash!"

Realizing the situation we were still in, I began crawling away as fast as I could. I continued pulling myself along until I heard a loud screech come from Cillian. I stopped and looked back to see he was bleeding from his neck. "Yes! You got him!"

Glen had to change guns since the rifle ran out of bullets. As he went to grab another, Cillian went after him, but was stopped by Roman. "YES!" I yelled from the top of my lungs. Roman got him down and pounded at his wound, making it bleed more and more. Kaden finally got up and shouted, "Roman stop!"

Mid-punch, he looked up at him and said, "Why? This fucker doesn't deserve to live! And Dr. Park didn't say he needed him alive."

Kaden walked over. "You're right, he didn't, and I'm not stopping you from killing him, but that's not the way to do it. You know how we must die, especially him," pointing to Cillian. "We need to make sure he doesn't heal."

Coughing up blood, Cillian stated, "You can't kill me! I'm a fucking g …!"

Roman stood up, placed his foot over Cillian's throat, and pushed down. "Yeah, yeah, yeah. We'll see about that, asshole."

Cillian struggled. Kaden looked over at me. I was so thrilled, but at the same time so frightened and just absolutely sick to my stomach. "Don't look, sweetie."

I nodded and turned away. I heard Glen say, "Here, this should work," before I heard what sounded like cutting noises and Cillian gargling. I shook and cried. "It's over, it's finally over," I thought.

Moments later, I felt a hand on my shoulder. I jumped a little and looked up to see my handsome brother. "Hey, it's okay."

I no longer saw fire-red eyes, scorched-like skin, and the spikes on his head. No, instead I saw his beautiful brown eyes; his healthy, pink, smooth skin; and his short, luscious brown hair. "Glen!" I screeched. I reached up and wrapped my arms around his normal-sized neck. He sat down and held me as I wept in his arms. I truly had my brother back!

After a while, Roman and Kaden came up to us and asked, "You okay, hon?"

I looked up at them, tears streaming from my eyes, and said, "I'm much better now."

I let go of Glen and wiped my cheeks as Roman and Kaden knelt down beside us. Kaden rubbed my back. I started asking, "Is he …" They all nodded. "Are you sure?"

Roman replied, "As a doornail."

I tried looking over, but all three of them stopped me. Kaden said, "It's better if you don't look, hon. That's one thing you don't need to see."

I nodded. "I'll take your word for it."

Then both Kaden and Roman looked at Glen. Roman said, "So 'the cure' does work."

Glen nodded. "You'll experience a bright light for a little while, but yes, it works."

I became upset. "So you did die?!"

"Yeah, I was gone for maybe thirty seconds."

"And how the hell was I going to explain that to Mom and Dad if you didn't come back?"

We all laughed. He shrugged. "You would've thought of something."

I smiled, grabbed his hand, and held it. "I'm just glad you're okay, bro."

"Me too, sis, me too."

All of a sudden, from behind my boys, we heard, "Holy shit!"

We looked over to see Dr. Park. He was scanning the room, trembling with fear as he saw all the devastation Cillian caused. He may be a doctor, but when you see a normally squeaky-clean room splattered from ceiling to floor with blood—and I'm not exaggerating, somehow blood got to the ceiling, as well—you would freak out, too. I tried to get up and go over to him, but my ankle laughed at me and said, "No!"

"Shit. Can someone help me up?"

They all helped me at once—Glen grabbed my right arm, Kaden was behind me, and Roman grabbed my left. Kaden and Roman picked me up like I was a feather while Glen was going a little slower. "Oh, okay, I've got to remember I'm no longer as strong as I was." You could just see this wave of disappointment wash over his face.

I said, "Hey." He looked at me. "Don't ever think you're now weak because you're no longer 'mutated.' You've always been strong, and you always will be. *Never* forget that."

He smiled. "Thanks, Ash."

"Of course. I love you."

"I love you, too." We touched our foreheads together.

With all three boys helping, I hobbled over to Dr. Park, who was still in utter shock. I said, "Dr. Park." He kept on looking around. I shouted, "Dr. Park!" He looked at me, on the verge of tears. "Are you okay?"

He shook his head violently. "No. I …I … I didn't know what they created. If …if … if I knew what the serum did, I would've stopped them a long time ago."

We all gawked at him, shocked. I asked, "What do you mean 'if you knew?'"

"They came to me years ago asking for my help, but I … I turned them down. I help people, not create super-soldiers."

Roman said, "Wait a minute, Doc. You knew and you didn't do or say anything?"

"Who was I going to report them to? Plus, I didn't hear or see more about it, so I thought they moved on." He cried, "I'm sorry. I'm so sorry."

I placed my hand on his shoulder and gently said, "It's okay, Dr. Park. Like you said, you didn't know, and they weren't going to tell you, whether you helped them or not. You probably wouldn't have known until you saw it for yourself."

He nodded as he wiped away his tears. I couldn't fault him or be mad at him for knowing. He's an innocent bystander in all of this. All he wanted to do was help and I commend him for that.

He looked up at Glen, Roman, and Kaden, and apologized profusely. Kaden replied, "It's okay, Dr. Park. You now have a cure," panning over to Glen.

"Yeah, but he died. It was a miracle I was able to revive him."

I could tell what Roman and Kaden were thinking. I chimed in, "Um, no."

Roman started, "But …"

"Hell no! I almost lost my blood-brother, what makes you two think I would be okay with possibly losing my chosen brothers."

Kaden agreed. "She makes a good point."

Dr. Park, finally composing himself, said, "Please, give me a month or two, and I'll have it figured out."

I looked up at Roman who was looking at Kaden. They shrugged. Roman looked back at the doctor and said, "I've been waiting almost two years for this moment. What's another month or two."

I beamed, proud of Roman for making such a mature decision. Dr. Park smiled and said, "Thank you."

"No, thank you, Dr. Park. We know you can do this," Kaden responded.

Then Roman had to say, "If you need any of Cillian's blood …"

Glen, Kaden, and I shouted, "Roman!"

"What? He said it may contain an answer to all of this. I'm just saying."

Dr. Park intervened, "No, he's right. I would like to see Cillian's body and take some samples."

As Roman walked over with Dr. Park, Kaden came around, gently grabbed my head, and placed it on his chest, knowing what I was about to do. "Please, hon, don't look."

Just from Dr. Park's reaction, I knew it was bad. As much as I wanted to see that son of a bitch's dead body, I didn't want to see what my boys did. They're not killers, they're protectors and did anything and everything to protect me.

After asking Roman to take the body to his office, he said, "Well, now what do we do? Who do we call?"

Being able to see again, I scanned around at the carnage Cillian left behind. It was absolutely revolting. "We can't leave them here."

"Dr. Park, is there a higher-up you may know of that we can call?" Kaden questioned.

He shook his head. Suddenly, we heard a moan come from behind us. We looked over and saw Sergeant Major O'Hare. He was slightly moving. We went (I hobbled) over to check on him. He had blood all over him. Whether it was his or not, we weren't 100% sure.

Dr. Park examined him. He checked for a pulse. "He's alive!" he exclaimed, looking up at us. I placed a hand over my mouth, so happy to hear he was still living. Dr. Park asked, "Sergeant Major, can you hear me?" He didn't reply. Dr. Park grabbed his hand. "Sergeant Major, if you can hear me, grip my hand."

We saw him somewhat grasp it. I gasped in joy. *Oh, thank God!*

Dr. Park continued scrutinizing him to see if the blood was his, where it was coming from, if he had any broken bones, and so on. He, at one point, must've hit a very tender spot near the Sergeant Major's ribs on his right side because when he did, the Sergeant Major actually yelled and moved. "So sorry, Sergeant Major. You definitely have what seem to be broken ribs. I need to get you to my actual office to properly examine you, do x-rays, and such."

Sergeant Major mumbled something, but none of us heard or understood him. Dr. Park leaned in closer to his mouth. "I'm sorry, Sergeant Major, what was that?"

"Call Sergeant Ramirez."

"Sergeant Ramirez?!" I shouted. "He's alive?!"

"Ashlynn, stay with Sergeant Major O'Hare. I'm going to run to my office and try calling Sergeant Ramirez."

I sat down, my legs outstretched, so I wasn't sitting on my bad ankle, and grabbed Sergeant Major's hand. "It's going to be okay, Sergeant Major." He gripped my hand, acknowledging me. I began to cry some more, not sad tears or fearful tears, but happy tears. Thankfully, two people I respected are alive. Cillian didn't get to them. Granted, the sergeant major was in a ton of pain, but he's alive and I know Dr. Park will take good care of him.

AUGUST 30th

It's been a little over two months since the horror at Lake Minnetaha ended. Sergeant Major is doing well. He definitely had some broken ribs, a concussion, and some bumps and bruises from, as he said, "Being thrown around by Cillian." Unfortunately, no other soldiers or workers that were in the building that day survived.

When Sergeant Ramirez and the rest of Sergeant Major's troops arrived at the building, they immediately went to their commander, got him on a gurney, and sent him somewhere. It wasn't Dr. Park's office, but I don't think it was a public hospital, either. It must've been a private facility for the army—for this particular group of soldiers, if you catch my drift. Sergeant Ramirez and I even embraced once the sergeant major was on his way, our minds at ease that this was finally over.

I've been staying in contact with Sergeant Major O'Hare. Once he was released, he went back, with his troops, to Lake Minnetaha to find any remaining creatures. He told me, "We will tell them a cure is being worked on. If they decide to receive the cure and go back to normal life, we will bring them back to the white building and take care of them."

I said, "Please tell me you're not going to put them in cages or those safe rooms."

"No, no, we're going to take offices and make them into rooms, so they can be comfortable."

"Oh, good." I paused for a moment. "And what about

any who decide to fight back?"

With a heavy heart, he replied, "I'm afraid we're going to have to execute them; especially if they decide to attack us."

I didn't exactly like hearing that, but I agreed. "Understood, Sergeant Major."

There's one other thing I will never forget from that day. When Sergeant Ramirez brought myself and Glen back to the cabin, we saw Jack standing outside with Chad, Greg, and Jerry, waiting for me to come home. Before the car fully stopped, I limped out and held onto the love of my life. I don't know who was squeezing harder because neither of us could breathe, but we didn't care, and we weren't letting go. We sobbed together, extremely happy and grateful that the hell was over.

After we were done hugging and crying, he looked up and was astonished to see Glen. "Holy shit, dude! You're you again!"

Glen laughed. "Yeah, and it feels damn good."

We stayed a few days, waiting for everything to de-escalate a bit and for my ankle to heal. Thankfully, it is doing better, but it's still messed up. Even Dr. Park said that it's probably something I will be living with for the rest of my life, but at least I can say I walked away from this frightening experience somewhat unscathed.

The night before we left, Kaden and Roman were over. I told them that I would gladly stay and be by their side as they waited for Dr. Park to "perfect" the cure. Kaden said, "No, hon. It's okay. You should go home and rest."

"But I am home," I replied.

He glared at me. "You know what I mean."

Glen stepped in and said, "Well, how about I stay here,

for now, until you guys are cured. I gotta figure things out anyway."

We all agreed that was a great idea, but, miraculously, we all didn't have to wait long. A couple of weeks ago, Glen called me on video chat–something we did every so often just to see each other, so I thought nothing of it. After going through the normal pleasantries of asking each other how we're doing and how we're feeling, he said, "I have a surprise for you." He rotated the screen and in front of me stood Roman and Kaden in their normal form.

I screamed, "It's my boys!"

Roman responded, "No, babe, it's your men," and flexed.

We all laughed. Glen put the tablet down and stood it up, so he could be in the shot, as well. I was so overjoyed to see all three of my brothers as themselves. I, of course, asked, "Did you guys ... die?"

Kaden answered, "Nope! Dr. Park improved the cure, so we didn't die!"

I became elated. "Oh my gosh, that's great! But how? What did he do to make it better?"

Roman said, "I don't know, hon. He rambled on about something having to do with Cillian's blood."

My eyes widened. "Really?!"

"Yeah, I didn't really pay attention, though, or care."

I rolled my eyes. "Kaden, please tell me you listened."

He laughed. "I'm sorry, sweetie, but I didn't. Once he mentioned that the cure was working and he was ready to test it on us, I kind of shut him out, as well."

"You?! Really?! The sensible one out of all of us and you didn't pay attention to *that*!" He smiled and shrugged. "Ugh! I'll just call Dr. Park and ask him myself. I'm curious to know."

We then decided that Jack and I would go up to the cabin, so we could all see each other—one last hoorah, if you will, before we all go on to live our lives. We decided to get together on August 30th (today), the same day that would've been our last day of vacation two years ago. Figured it would be kind of a bittersweet end to all of this chaos. I even suggested we invite my parents up, which they loved.

Then, the day after I talked to them, I took probably the most important test of my life. When the results came up, I called Jack over to me. "Yeah, babe. What's up?"

I said, "Look."

He looked and his eyes brightened. "Wait … are you telling me …"

"We're pregnant."

He hollered and scooped me up. He held me and we cried. "We're going to be parents," he mumbled into my neck. Then he gently put me down, realizing, "Wait, if you're finding out now that you're pregnant, does that mean …"

My heart dropped a bit and I nodded. "I was most likely pregnant when everything was going on."

Jack became extremely concerned. "Do you think the baby is okay? Do you think anything happened?"

Before he spat out any more questions that I had no answers to, I placed my fingers over his lips and said, "Baby, I'm sure it's fine, but we won't know until we see the doctor."

"Which probably won't be until after we travel."

"Exactly."

"Well, then we're driving up. We're not flying. I don't want to take any risks."

I chuckled. "Babe, I'm sure it's safe for me to fly. Besides, it is a good ten-hour drive from here to the cabin."

"Then we'll rent an RV, so you can be comfy. I don't care, I just want to make sure you and," he gently placed his hand on my belly, "the baby are safe."

I grinned, just feeling love enveloping me. I couldn't believe how lucky I was to have such an amazing, supportive, and protective man in my life.

****

We left to head up to the cabin the morning of August 28th–early in the morning, which I was not happy about–and we got there that evening. I wanted to get there a day early, so I could have some time with my boys before my parents came and I'm glad we did. We talked, we laughed, we walked through the woods (which felt so good to do and not feel like we were being watched), we swam in the lake (which felt even better), and just had an amazing time. Truly like the good ol' days!

The thing is, I told my boys and my parents what we were doing–taking an RV up–but not why we were doing it. As far as they knew, we weren't flying because Jack and I were getting ready to do a lot of traveling for the show, so we didn't want to put any more stress on our bodies. Hey, they bought it! But I did get sick yesterday morning and this morning, so things started looking suspicious to Glen and Kaden. Not Roman, though. He was completely oblivious.

My parents got to the cabin this afternoon, so Jack and I decided the best time to tell them would be after dinner. It killed me having this secret and not saying anything, but I knew when we finally did tell them, it would be totally worth it. Plus, Charlie joined us, so my parents got to meet him, as well, and he would get to join in the festivities of finding out he, too, would become an uncle soon.

Once we finished eating and cleaning up, we all continued sitting at the dining room table, talking. *Perfect!*

However, my dad asked, "So, what are you all going to do now that you're 'back to normal?'"

Damn!

He panned over to Kaden and Charlie. "Boys, do you have anything planned?"

They looked at each other and Kaden swallowed before answering. "Well, Dad, we were looking to stay in the area."

"Really?!" we all exclaimed in unison.

He looked around at all of us. "Yeah. I mean, what I went through here wasn't pleasant, but this is the type of place I've been looking for–quiet, peaceful. I fell in love with it the second we got here two years ago, and I knew then that I didn't want to leave. Now that I've met Charlie ..." They looked at each other and smiled with so much love. They reminded me of Jack and I, and I loved it! "... I really don't want to leave."

My dad inquired, "Charlie, do you agree?"

"I do."

Roman just had to chime in, "Then I pronounce you husband and husband. You may kiss your husband."

We all laughed, but Kaden and Charlie's was more nervous than jovial. It looked like they had something on their minds, but they didn't know how to say it, or were too nervous to say it. My father continued, "So then, Kaden and Charlie, do you have a place picked out?"

Kaden and Charlie looked at each other, again very nervous. Kaden nodded to him and turned back toward my father. He said, "Well, we were hoping to stay here at the cabin."

My parents were flabbergasted. I actually yelled out,

"What?!"

Kaden got scared. "What I mean is, we would like to be the caretakers of the cabin. We would watch over it and keep it clean. We wouldn't be its homeowners. We would never take that away from you. I just …"

My father smiled. "It's okay, Kaden. We're not mad. We're just shocked, that's all."

Kaden was so relieved. You could see tears welling up in his eyes, which made tears well up in mine. "I'm sorry, we didn't mean to upset you, but this cabin really feels like home to me, to us."

Roman stated, "That may be because you've been living around it for two years." I slapped him. "Ow! What?! I'm just saying!"

I shook my head. My dad said to Kaden, "Son, you know that our home, whether this cabin or our house in Florida, is your home. We just ask that when we want to come here for some downtime, since it is safe now, we're allowed back."

Charlie answered, "Oh my gosh, of course, Mr. Amuso. We'll …"

Oh, shit! Here we go!

My mom interjected, "Excuse me, Charlie. I know you're new here, but there's no such thing as Mr. and Mrs. Amuso. It's Mom and Dad, okay, sweetie?"

Charlie began to cry. "I thought I would never use those words again. Thank you for being so kind."

My mom grabbed his hand. "You're very welcome, honey. Thank you for showing love to a man who thought he couldn't be loved because of the way he looked."

Charlie and Kaden looked at each other and beamed.

My dad said, "Okay, well Kaden is set. What about you,

Glen? What are your plans, son?"

Glen became sheepish. "Honestly, Dad, I was kind of hoping to move back in with you and Mom for a little bit. Get a job in Florida and start over."

My mom asked, "Don't take this the wrong way, Glenny, because I would love to have you back, but you don't want to go back to New York or *Replay*?"

"Nah. As much as I loved working there, New York was too cold for me."

We all laughed again. My dad said, "That's fine, Glen. You can move back in with us until you get your feet back under you."

Glen smiled. "Thanks, Dad."

My father nodded. "And you, Roman? What are your plans?"

Roman looked down. "I … I don't really know yet."

My mom rubbed his shoulder and said, "And that's okay, sweetie. You went through a traumatic experience. You don't need to have all the answers right now."

Roman appreciated her response, but I could tell he was hurting. I wanted to talk to him about it, but figured tonight wasn't the right time. *I'll grab him tomorrow!*

Now, it was my turn. "Hey, there's something we need to show you guys." I said, trying to be serious.

Kaden looked over and asked, "Is everything okay, hon?"

"Well, we found something, and we wanted to show you guys. See if you recognize it."

"You mean another creature?"

"Well, you can kind of say that."

Everyone looked at me with confusion and concern until I placed the pregnancy test on the table. It took them a second to process what they were looking at. My mom was, of course, the first to understand and she screamed at the top of her lungs, jumped up, and ran over to me. I met her halfway and we held each other tightly as we cried. "My baby is having a baby!"

After holding on to each other, I let go to then hug my father. "I'm so happy for you, princess."

"Thank you, Daddy."

"Are you feeling okay?"

"Just some morning sickness, but otherwise I'm good."

Glen shouted, "I knew something was up when you got sick yesterday and this morning! 'Car ride sickness' my ass!"

We all laughed once more. I went over to him. "Come here, Uncle Glen!"

I went around hugging everyone as they congratulated Jack and me. As I hugged Charlie, he said, "I'm so happy for you, sweetie."

I replied, "Thank you, Uncle Charlie."

He let go of me and held me at arm's length with this surprised expression on his face. He said, "I'm sorry?"

"Dude, you're a part of this family now, so, yes, you will be Uncle Charlie."

He cried some more as he hugged me again. He and Kaden had similar situations where their families deserted them when they came out, so upon hearing he has a family again ... well, of course he was going to cry–happy tears.

AUGUST 31st

This morning, we woke up to the delicious smell of breakfast being made, which made me sick. "Oh, this sucks," I whined to my husband.

"I know, I'm sorry, babe. But just think, in what, seven or eight months it'll all be worth it."

I looked up at him and bore a hole into him. "I love you, but ..." and vomited again. "This is your fault."

He chuckled. "I'm going to have you give me a nickel every time you say that. I may be a rich man by the time you have the baby."

I couldn't help but laugh at that. Then we heard a knock at the door. "You okay, sweetheart?"

"Yeah, Mom, I'm fine."

"Okay, honey. Once you're done, come out and eat."

"Ma, I don't think I can eat anything right now."

"Oh, you say that now."

And wouldn't you know it, my mom was right. After throwing up whatever I ate yesterday, I was ready to eat anything and everything put in front of me. "So this is pregnancy, huh?"

My mom laughed. "Oh, wait until you get into the second and third trimesters. Your cravings will start getting really weird."

"Oh, goody. I can't wait."

We ate and enjoyed breakfast. While everyone worked on

cleaning up, I grabbed Roman. "Can we talk for a second?"

"Absolutely."

We went outside and sat by the lake. I wrapped my arms around his big ol' arm and leaned on it. "Brings back some memories, huh?"

He tittered. "Yeah, one of my favorites."

I looked at him. "Really?!"

He looked at me. "Yeah. We were finally back together. How can that not be one of my favorite memories?"

I smiled. "True." I waited a moment before asking, "So, what *is* next for you, Roman? Are you going back down to Mexico to find all those girls you talked about?"

He frowned. "You know that's a front, babe. I have no one. Not even my parents care about me."

I let go of his arm and grabbed his hand. "Don't say that Roman." He looked at me. "You are so loved, and you are wanted. You may be an asshole, but you're *my* asshole." We laughed. "And there is someone out there waiting for you to find them."

"You think so?"

"I know so, bud."

He smiled. "To be honest, I was thinking about going back to New York and going back to *Replay*, but I don't know if Mr. Schneider will take me back."

"Why wouldn't he?"

"He probably found someone better to replace me. And I know I wasn't his favorite."

"Well, yeah, let's face it, I was the favorite out of all of us." He rolled his eyes and chuckled. "But I've stayed in contact with him, and he constantly asks about you guys, especially you."

He looked up at me, astonished. "Really?!"

"Yeah! He loved you, Roman! And he said that if any of us, especially you, wanted to come back, the door was always open."

He beamed. "Yes!"

"Then I guess you know what you're doing?"

"I'm going back to New York, baby!"

"Yay!" I gave him a hug. I was so proud of him. I feel like we've just been a huge part of his life for so long that him going off and "being on his own" was a pretty big accomplishment. However, we all reminded him–after he made his announcement–that if he ever needs anything, we're only a phone call and a flight away.

We continued having a wonderful day while Jack and I worked on packing everything up as we were leaving in the morning. I had a doctor's appointment on the third to see how the baby's doing and how far along I am. Then we start traveling for the show.

As much as it broke my heart to leave, it also felt good knowing my boys were themselves and ready to face the world anew.

SEPTEMBER 3rd

Today was the doctor's appointment and it went a lot better than we expected. We found out I was about ten weeks in, and the baby was looking healthy. We did mention to the doctor what happened within the first couple of weeks of me being pregnant before finding out. We explained that a deranged fan stalked me and attacked me–which wasn't 100% a lie. The doctor said, "We'll keep an eye on this little one, but right now, everything looks really good. I would just say don't do anything too strenuous."

Jack and I looked at each other. I said, "We're about to travel for our show."

She responded, "Jack may be traveling for the show, but you're not." Both of our faces dropped to the floor. "I'm sorry, Ashlynn, but after what you just told me, I would rather you stay home and rest than travel around the world."

Jack reluctantly agreed. "It makes sense, but I don't want to leave you home alone."

I thought for a second and then smiled. "Don't worry. I won't be."

As soon as we got home from the appointment, I called up Mr. Scarlo and told him the news. He squealed so loud the neighborhood dogs started barking. "Aw, sweetie, I'm so excited for you two!"

"Thank you, Mr. Scarlo. But I do have a massive favor to ask."

"Of course, honey, anything."

"Jack has to go travel for the show and I'm 'grounded' because I was pregnant when everything happened in Lake Minnetaha."

He gasped. "Oh my goodness! Is the baby okay?"

"Yes, the baby is looking good, but my doctor doesn't want me to put any extra stress on me or the baby, just to be safe."

I didn't have to say anymore. Mr. Scarlo knew what I was asking before I even said anything. "Don't worry, sweetie. When is Jack leaving?"

"Next week."

"David and I will be there with Mr. Bojangles. We'll stay for as long as you need us to."

I heard David in the background. "I'm sorry, what am I doing?"

He must've just walked in. Mr. Scarlo explained, "We're going to Ashlynn's place and watching her while her husband travels."

"Why?"

"Because she's pregnant and she got pregnant when…"

"Say no more. When are we leaving?"

We figured out dates and everything before I said, "Thank you, Mr. Scarlo. I truly appreciate it. Oh, and please, none of your tea."

"Honey, I'm not *that* stupid. I know not to give my tea to a pregnant woman."

We laughed. At least I know while Jack's away I'll have some of the best—and cutest—company ever. No, seriously, Mr. Bojangles is the most handsome puppy to walk this earth. Yeah, I probably should've asked my parents, but as much as

I love them, I moved out for a reason. I need my space, and with me being pregnant, my mom would be on me like bees to honey, asking me every two seconds if I needed anything, if I was okay, and so on. I need to relax, and who better to help with that than the "relax master" himself.

MARCH 17th

Baby girl is here! Our daughter, Gabriella Nancy, was born on March 15th after a very long labor. Everyone–from Mom and Dad; to Kaden and Charlie; to Glen and his girlfriend, Denise; to Roman and his girlfriend (yup, you read that right), Piper– were all there to greet her. Honestly, seeing Roman holding his niece was probably the most precious thing ever, but seeing my husband hold his daughter made me fall in love with him even more. I could see that he was ready to do anything and everything for her. She's going to be daddy's little girl.

We just got home this morning. My mom and dad will be staying for the next few weeks (they joked, saying, "Maybe even a few months;" however, I don't think they were kidding), but Glen, Kaden, Roman, and their partners were staying until tomorrow as they had to get back to work. Glen, Kaden, Roman, and I, along with Gabriella, were sitting in my living room talking when I said, "I know we don't have the luxury of a two-month vacation anymore …"

Roman chimed in, "I do," with a shit-eating grin on his face.

We loud whispered, "Shut up, Roman," so we didn't bother the baby. She cooed in my arms and moved around a bit.

Roman got up and came over to me. "Give me my niece. She's not going to yell at me for no reason."

We all laughed. He gently grabbed her, put her in his

arms, and sat back down. I joked, "Yeah, yeah. She's not yelling at you, *yet*." We laughed again. "But in all seriousness, guys, I want us to continue our yearly vacation, even if it's for a week or two. We can bring our partners. I will, of course, bring Gabriella …."

Glen interjected, "You better bring my niece, or I'm not coming."

I glared at him, smiling. He loves his niece already. "And we'll have fun, like we used to."

Kaden piped up, "I love this idea!"

Glen and Roman agreed. I said, "Great! I figured we could go to …"

All three said in unison, "Woah, woah, woah, you're not picking."

I was shocked and a little hurt. "Why not?"

Roman replied while rocking Gabriella, "Uh, because we're not having a repeat of Lake Minnetaha."

I was about to say something, but realized they were right. "Fair enough." I sulked.

Kaden said, "Ashlynn, we love you dearly, but hell no."

I couldn't help but laugh. Glen asked, "So whose turn is it anyway to pick?"

We all thought for a moment, literally trying to remember whose turn it was, when I saw a lightbulb go off in Kaden's head. He said, "Why don't we have Gabriella pick each year from now on?"

Roman shouted, "What?!"

Gabriella started crying. "Oh, you scared her!" I exclaimed.

Glen shot up. "Here, let me have my niece. I'll calm her down."

Kaden argued, "Well, wait a minute, I haven't held her yet today."

I said, "Guys!" They all looked at me. "My daughter isn't a hot potato."

They apologized as Glen took her and she did start calming down. He smiled. "See. I have the magic touch."

We all rolled our eyes. I asked, "So does that mean you're going to live here and get up with her when she cries in the middle of the night?"

"Nope."

I snapped my fingers. "Damn, I tried."

We laughed once again. I then looked at Kaden. "To go back to our vacation discussion, I can't believe I'm about to say this, but I have to agree with Roman. How the hell is she going to pick where we go?"

Kaden answered, "Jack has a globe here, right?"

"Yeah, in his office."

"We'll spin it, place her finger on it, and wherever it lands, that's where we'll go."

Glen, Roman, and I looked at each other as our eyes widened with joy. "Holy shit, that's brilliant!" I declared.

"Yeah, I love this idea! Right, babe?" Glen said, looking down at Gabriella.

"I'm in!" Roman stated.

"All right, let's head upstairs."

Glen carried his niece as we all went to Jack's office. *Okay, Gabriella, where are we headed to next?*

Acknowledgements

In February 2022, I published my first book *The Disappearance* all on my own. It was nerve-racking and I was scared of what the outcome might be, but I am so proud of what I did. I am also very happy to say that the response has been great!

Now, a little over a year later, I'm publishing my second book, *He's Here!*, the sequel to *The Disappearance*, and I am, once again, very proud of myself. The mental blocks, the searches for a different word other than "said" or "laughed," the plethora of times I cried wondering if I'm doing the right thing are so worth it because I am still living my dream.

However, this wouldn't be happening without the help and support of so many.

To my mom, Connie, and my brother, Anthony (aka Butthead). Truly thank you for sticking by my side and never belittling my dreams. Because of your constant belief in me and pushing me, I am where I am today.

To my family—my aunts and uncles, my cousins, my in-laws, and my nephews. Thank you for your continued love and support as I pursue my writing career.

To my chosen family, my best friends who have stood by my side during the best of times and the worst; thank you, thank you, THANK YOU! I love you all SO much! You are my family because you have done so much for me throughout our time together and I don't think these words express how much I appreciate you!

To my readers: Barbara Dickinson, Elisa Fries, George Adams, Heather Hodorovych, and Louise Stahl. Because of you all taking the time out of your crazy days to read through my story to make sure everything was looking good and sounding good, it is the masterpiece it is today. Thank you from the bottom of my heart!

To my amazing fans on my Facebook page who have been following me since day one, supporting me, and watching my Live Reading Wednesday streams every Wednesday at 7:15pm (EST). Thank you for being so loving and caring to someone you don't really know, but follow because you love my writing, you think I'm funny, you think I'm weird, or whatever the case may be. You guys are THE BOMB DOT COM! I love you all!

To my dear uncle, Mark Bailey. You did it again! This cover is so beautiful! I had no clue what I wanted, and it showed with the back-and-forth messages we had. But you took the little suggestions I made and turned them into a cover I never foresaw and better than I could ever imagine. Thank you!

To my beautiful angels in Heaven: Nanny, Poppy, Grandpa Hodorovych, my sisters, Valerie and Angela, and my father, George. I miss you and love you all so much. I continue to hope and pray that I've made you all proud.

Lastly, to the man who has stood by my side and cheered me on since day one. To the man who whenever I wanted to give up, pushed me harder than ever. To the man I love more than anything. Thank you, John, for not only being the best husband EVER, but for being the one I could celebrate even the tiniest victories with and make it feel like the biggest. To being the one who would take the brunt of my anger and help me calm down. To being the one I could cry to. I love you so much, baby! We did it again! Here's to many more!

A Special Shout-Out

I want to give a special shout-out to my late aunt-in-law, Janice Foley. Aunt Janice, if it wasn't for you wondering if Dr. Park was more involved with the experiments, I don't think he would be in this book. I had a different ending in mind that wasn't as good as the one in here. That change happened because of you. Thank you for the inspiration!

It breaks my heart that you won't get to see this book, but I know you're looking down, (hopefully) happy that Dr. Park made it in.

About the Author

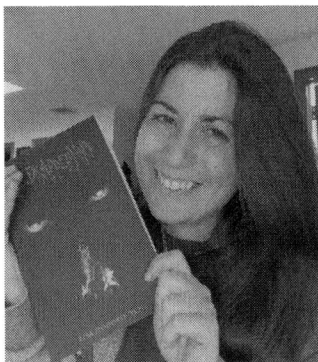

Writing has always been a constant for Lisa. Ever since she was little, she knew she was going to be an author and she's been living her dream since 2022.

When she's not working on her own writing, she's either working with others on their stories through her company, Quoth the Writer, or she's posting book reviews, tea reviews, or Godzilla discussions on her social media.

She currently lives in New Jersey with her husband, John. When she's not working or writing, she's either watching her favorite movies or TV shows, reading, or spending time with her family, friends, and husband.

Facebook: @LisaHodorovych or @QuoththeWriter
Instagram: @thewriterslife87 or @quoththewriter18

Reminder: Please leave a review, whether good or bad, on GoodReads, Amazon, and/or your social media. If you do leave a review on Facebook or Instagram, please make sure to tag me in it. Thank you again in advance!

Made in the USA
Middletown, DE
28 June 2023

34043807R00104